Allen & Un   ...s to bring
Australia's   ...u literary heritage to a
broad audience by creating affordable print and
ebook editions of the nation's most significant
and enduring writers and their work. The fiction,
non-fiction, plays and poetry of generations of
Australian writers that were published before the
advent of ebooks will now be available to new
readers, alongside a selection of more recently
published books that had fallen out of circulation.

The House of Books is an eloquent collection
of Australia's finest literary achievements.

Kenneth Cook was born in Sydney in 1929. He achieved recognition as a fiction writer with the publication of his first novel, *Wake in Fright*, in 1961. Critically acclaimed, it has been translated into several languages and is still in print today. It was made into a classic Australian film in 1971.

Wake in Fright was followed by over twenty fiction and non-fiction books, including *Eliza Frazer*, *Bloodhouse*, *Tuna* and *Pig*. His antiwar beliefs were reflected in his powerful novel *The Wine of God's Anger* and in the play *Stockade*. Kenneth Cook died of a heart attack in 1987 while on a publicity tour promoting *Wombat Revenge*, the second volume in his bestselling trilogy of humorous short stories.

A&U HOUSE *of* BOOKS

KENNETH COOK

Tuna

For Patricia

This edition published by Allen & Unwin House of Books in 2012
First published by Cheshire Publishing, Melbourne, in 1967

Allen & Unwin
Sydney, Melbourne, Auckland, London

83 Alexander Street
Crows Nest NSW 2065
Australia
Phone: (61 2) 8425 0100
Email: info@allenandunwin.com
Web: www.allenandunwin.com

Cataloguing-in-Publication details are available
from the National Library of Australia
www.trove.nla.gov.au

ISBN 978 1 74331 438 8 (pbk)
ISBN 978 1 74343 097 2 (ebook)

Printed and bound in Australia by the SOS Print + Media Group.

1

The Italian threw the one hundred and fifty pound anchor over the bow and went straight over with it because his leg was tangled in the line. Two sudden splashes, a flurry of white on the green water and then just green water.

There were twenty fathoms underneath the keel. The anchor went straight down, with the Italian clawing for the green light he could see above him where the sun touched the surface of the water.

His two brothers saw him go. They ran to the bow and clutched futilely at the racing line. It ran stiffly down into the green sea with nothing to indicate that there was a man filling with water on the end of it.

The line stopped as the anchor hit the bottom. The two Italians tried to haul it up but it wouldn't move and one of the brothers ran back to the cabin to turn on the radio and scream for help.

A mile away, on the other side of the Marabell Light Island, a small fishing boat was drifting with the swell. Two men were sitting in the stern fishing for flathead, one was white, the other was black.

The white man, Jack Foster, hauled a five-pound flathead on to the deck, jerked the hook from its mouth and tossed the fish into a basket. There were three other fish already in the basket.

'That's two quid for the day,' said Foster. 'You're going to be bloody lucky to get your wages this week.'

The black man grinned dutifully.

'I'll get five times as much as you before the day's out.'

'I wouldn't bet on it,' said Foster.

The black man pulled in his line and re-baited with a chunk of red tuna flesh. He dropped the baited hook over the side and the sea ran away with the line, drawing it out from the boat until the lead hit the bottom with a gentle bump.

Both men were stripped to the waist. Foster was burned a deep copper red by the sun. He sat on the hatch cover, his back bent so that the broad, flat muscles of his stomach formed three hard ridges. He was not much taller than the wiry black man but he was three times as big around the shoulders and chest.

He looked to the starboard where a series of basalt rocks, running out in a tiny archipelago, stretched to the south of the Marabell Island.

The black man laughed.

'What's funny, Bill?' asked Foster.

'I was just thinking of those rocks,' said the black man. 'We pulled a bloke and his wife off there last year when I was fishing with Jimmy Evans.'

Bill laughed again and began pulling his line in.

'Well, come on,' said Foster. 'What's funny about that?'

'Well, this bloke had been out in a dinghy and he'd lost an oar. The dinghy bumped into the rock, that last one on the end there it was, and they both hopped out on to it and let the dinghy go, and there was the pair of them stuck like a couple of pelicans on a rock.'

Foster laughed.

'Yeah, but that's not all,' said Bill. 'This bloke hung on to the one oar you see. He was wearing trunks and his wife had on a pair of white slacks. So he makes her take them off and he ties the trousers up to the oar and he stands there waving 'em in the air.'

Foster laughed again.

'Well,' said Bill, dropping his line, 'me and Jimmy Evans sees him and go across to him and the bloke gets so excited he drops the oar. So we picks up him and mum and takes them back to town with mum in her underpants.'

Bill laughed uncontrollably at the memory.

'And the way that bloke swore at us. God, you never heard anything like it. You'd think *we'd* lost his wife's pants. He abused us all the way back to town.'

Three miles to the west on the high hill by the seaside on which the township of Bernadine was perched, a policeman was trying to understand the terrified garble of Italian and English which sprayed over him through a

3

radio receiver.

'Listen,' said the policeman. 'Listen to me Speak slower and in English if you can.'

Again the incomprehensible stream carrying with it somehow the urgency of terror.

The policeman walked out to the front door of the police station and on to the verandah which overlooked the sea. North and south the shoreline ran for fifty miles in receding masses of blue hills fringed by white half-ovals of sand, then the sharper white of the line of surf from the breakers, and then the countless square miles of blue-green sea.

The Marabell Light Island lay due east and the policeman could see two boats, one to the north of the island, one to the south. The northern boat was a stranger but the southern boat came from Bernadine and the policeman knew it.

He went back inside and manipulated the radio.

'Police at Bernadine calling the *Elsie*. Police at Bernadine calling the *Elsie*. Do you receive me, Jack?'

'I'm receiving you, Rod,' said Foster.

'Jack,' said the policeman. 'I'm getting a funny sort of call. I think it's from a boat on the other side of the island from you and they seem to be in trouble of some sort but I can't understand them. Could you go and have a look?'

'Who is it?' said Foster.

'Don't know,' said the policeman, and added non-committedly, 'Italians.'

He would have said dagoes but the last time he had called Italians dagoes somebody had complained to Headquarters and he had been told not to do it.

Foster knew what he meant anyway.

4

'Pull up, Bill,' said Foster. 'There's some dago in trouble over there.'

Bill didn't answer. He began quickly pulling in the heavy nylon lines, coiling them expertly on the deck. By the time he finished Foster had the motor going and had turned the small launch northwest through the calm water. Bill dropped a fishing basket on each of the lines to stop the wind tangling them and swung down from the bow to the cabin with Foster.

'What's wrong?' he asked.

'Don't know. Dagoes.'

Bill grunted.

There were few men to whom Bill felt himself superior, but dagoes were unquestionably amongst these few. His own place in the fishing society in which he lived was distinctly below that of a white. It was accepted that he didn't need the things a white man needed, that it was normal for him not to set up a house and family, that he should have no aspirations towards property or success. But Bill accepted this, too, as casually and inevitably as the white man. They would drink with him, eat with him, talk to him without ever deferring to his point of view, and accept him as part of their society. It never occurred to them or Bill to think of superiority or inferiority. He was just there.

But Bill regarded himself as an altogether different species from the dagoes. They had foreign ways and lived within themselves and if they could speak the language at all spoke it indistinctly with strange accents. These things alone made Bill think of them as infinitely inferior to himself. But then they had brought their strange, foreign fishing habits to the traditionally Australian

5

grounds of the south coast; they were less than men.

If Bill had been able to put all this into words his white associates would have agreed with him. As it was the sentiments of all concerned were summed up in the term 'dagoes'.

'Get up and see if you can see them,' said Foster.

Bill swung over the cabin, climbed up the roof and stood swaying with the light movement of the boat. Just ahead lay the island, five square miles of rock and coarse grass inhabited by rabbits, goats, seals, two lighthouse keepers and their families.

The sea was empty apart from a cloud of seagulls fluttering whitely and nervously in the lee of the island.

Bill dropped back into the cabin.

'Must be on the other side,' he said.

Foster cut in close around the island's northwest point. The seals that lived in the rocky bay came tumbling over the rocks. The cows went plunging into the water and swam out amiably. The bulls stayed ponderously on the edge of the rocks and glowered morosely.

Foster saw the Italians' boat apparently anchored two hundred yards off the island. Two men on the bow were hauling at the anchor rope.

'Can't see anything wrong,' said Bill.

'If the silly bastards have called me out because they've caught their anchor I'll kick their guts in,' said Foster.

He was puzzled. There was something wrong with the tableau of the two men on the bow of their boat struggling frantically with the anchor rope.

'What *is* wrong with the silly bastards?'

'I don't know,' said Bill. 'They look upset about something though.'

6

Foster came around the stern of the Italians' boat and handed the wheel to Bill. 'Stay in close,' he said.

Foster moved out on to the bows and leapt across three feet of water to the stern of the Italian boat. His boots thudded on to the deck but his heavy body swayed easily with the shock.

The Italians were hanging on to the anchor rope and waving at him and shouting. Foster went forward and stood looking at them with his hands on his hips, a square, curiously Nordic figure contrasting strongly with the dark-faced Latins.

'What's wrong?' he said. But the Italians had lost their use of English. They could only shout and gesture at the innocent green water under the bows.

'What the hell's wrong?' said Foster.

One of the Italians thrust the anchor rope into Foster's hand and began to haul. Foster automatically leant on the rope and felt the leaden dragging movement. There was a soggy heaviness on the line, different from the sharp dead weight of an anchor.

'All right,' he said, 'so you've caught something in the anchor. So what. Haul it up.'

The Italians only gibbered, and Foster saw with disbelief that tears were streaming from the eyes of one of them.

Foster gave in and pulled steadily on the rope, cursing the Italians for their irregular jerky hauling. The anchor was coming up with a strange sideways slewing movement.

A flock of seagulls came screaming around the bows.

Foster saw the dark shape of the Italian on the end of the anchor rope.

7

Then a booted leg broke the water with the rope in a neat half-hitch around the ankle.

He understood with a surge of bitterness against the lunacy of all dagoes, bitterness against a man who could stand on a coiled anchor rope as he threw the anchor over, bitterness against the men who couldn't haul him up.

He pushed the Italians aside, leaned over the bows and turned the full strength of his shoulders and arms to trying to pull the Italian's head clear of the water.

'Haul, you bastards,' he screamed at the men behind him and felt their puny strengths take up on the rope.

He grabbed at the drowned man's ankle and cursed again as the body sank in the water when the full weight fell to the Italians.

He bent over the bows again and hauled the man almost clear of the water by his leg. His head was still under. Foster braced himself against the bow rails and held the body against the hull with his right hand. The muscles of his arm shook under the weight of the man and the anchor.

With his left hand he pulled the long-bladed gutting knife from his hip sheath and sliced through the thick wet rope below the half-hitch around the man's leg. The anchor fell away cleanly and the desperate weight on Foster's arm eased.

He dragged the body over the bows. It fell soggily on to the deck.

'How long's he been down?' he asked. But the Italians were standing limply against the cabin staring with stricken eyes at their brother.

'Shit,' said Foster, swinging the body around face-

8

downwards so the head lay towards the stern.

Water and mucus were running out of the man's nose and mouth.

Foster turned the head around.

The eyes were half open and there was good colour in the face. Foster didn't know whether it was because the man was half alive or because he was a dago.

He thrust his fingers into the Italian's mouth and caught the turned-back tongue, pulling it out from the throat. He pressed downwards at the man's back, put his arm under his legs and raised him and shook him. Water poured out through the mouth and ran down the deck between the tar lines.

Foster turned the body over on its back, closed the nostrils with the fore-finger and thumb of his left hand and shoved his own mouth over the wet slack lips of the Italian.

He blew and felt the nostrils expand under his fingers.

He came away and pressed down on the man's chest.

There was a watery gurgle in the body and something like a belch erupted through the passive mouth.

Foster covered the Italian's mouth with his own again and felt the stubble of the unshaven face cutting the inside of his lips. He blew hard but he could feel the air was not getting down past the throat.

He stood up and grabbed the man by the legs.

'Give us a hand, you stupid bastards,' he yelled at the two Italians still staring fearfully at him. But they wouldn't move.

Foster stood up with the drowned man's legs at either side of his head and shook the body violently. The rope was still around the man's ankle and Foster tore it free.

Some coins fell out of the Italian's pockets and rattled on to the deck. Water and mucus stained with blood poured from the gaping mouth. When it stopped Foster dropped the body on to the deck again and tried to blow air into the lungs.

He tried for twenty minutes and his own mouth was cut and bleeding from the stubble on the Italian's lips.

'Didn't the bastard ever shave?' he said as he finally gave up and, with a kind of shamed deference to the mystery, turned the body on its back and roughly crossed the hands on the sodden stomach.

Foster turned to the Italians still by the cabin.

'He's dead,' he said roughly. 'You better take him back.'

The men did not answer, they stood staring at the body. One of them was still crying. The other crept softly forward and knelt by the body. Quickly he crossed himself, then shook his head and stood up. He turned to Foster.

'He was our brother,' he said, staring despairingly with full wet eyes at Foster's face.

'Sorry,' said Foster, embarrassed. 'You better take him back—we're getting close to the island.'

The boat had been drifting towards the rocks ever since the anchor had come up.

'You take us back please,' said the Italian softly.

Foster looked at the body and the two broken men on the deck and shrugged. He turned towards his own boat.

'I'll take it in, Bill,' he shouted. 'You follow me.'

He pushed open the door of the cabin, worked the starter and the throttle and heard with satisfaction the strong growl of the diesel. He turned the wheel over away from the island, put the gear in and pushed the throttle forward.

The Italians scrambled into the cabin with him.

'One of you better stay out there with him,' said Foster, but they both huddled on to a bench and didn't answer.

Foster turned the boat right around and headed towards the Bernadine Bar three miles away.

The radio was still on and the mouthpiece swung idly where the Italians had dropped it. Foster picked it up.

'*Elsie* calling police at Bernadine,' he said. '*Elsie* calling police at Bernadine.'

A distorted voice came over the radio. 'Rod Armstrong here, Jack. I can hear you. What happened?'

'Bloke threw himself over with the anchor,' said Foster. 'He's dead. Two others on board. I'm bringing them back to Bernadine.'

'O.K., Jack.'

By now, Foster knew, most of the people in Bernadine would be on the hotel verandah overlooking the sea and the entrance to the port. They'd watch as the boat came in, then they'd all troop down to the wharves to meet them.

The hotel was at the top of a hill overlooking a tall spit of rock which shielded the entrance to the river. A bar of sand went out from the rock and changed on every tide. The surf rolled across the bar and the fishing boats had to come in through the surf and turn sharply up into the river. It was all right on a quiet day and this was a quiet day, although the sea had risen since Foster had left that morning.

He felt the tension draining from his body. Bill was keeping pace with him on the starboard side. He could see the dark broad face of the aborigine looking curiously across at him.

Foster felt a half-admitted cold envy that two lunatic dagoes should own a boat like this, forty feet long with a powerful diesel, a broad beam and plenty of deck space. A boat like this would hold ten tons of tuna. His own boat was so small it wasn't even worth using to fish tuna.

He looked at the two Italians. One, the one who had been crying, had a harsh craggy face like a Roman soldier's. The other was a soft-looking, big-eyed man. Both of them were sitting with their hands hanging down, not speaking.

A boat like this would cost you five thousand pounds thought Foster. His own had cost him seven hundred and fifty.

Where did the bastards get the money anyway?

The boat came out of the shelter of the island and began to rock a little. Foster looked out towards the bar across the body of the Italian on the bows. The man's head was beginning to roll from side to side.

'One of you better get out there and look after him,' Foster said to the Italians. 'Someone will have to hold him when we're going through the surf.'

One of the Italians raised his head, then shook it sorrowfully from side to side. The other didn't move.

Foster left the wheel, went up to the bows and caught the body by the heels. He dragged it backwards down towards the stern and jammed it between the cabin and the side rails with a fishing basket. The man's arms trailed up behind his head as he was dragged along and Foster was going to leave them like that then he changed his mind and crossed them on the stomach again.

The boat was running along by the rocky shore now where the blue water broke white on the black granite rock.

As with many southern New South Wales fishing villages the port was actually in the river. At Bernadine the port was half a mile upstream. The river ran down from the wharves, then turned a right angle to run along the inside of the spit of rock and then into the sea. Where sea and river met there was always rough water. If the surf were running high the water was very rough. There was always a bar of sand and it was the constant conflict of the two bodies of water that made the bar change position so often.

Foster turned the wheel so that the boat came broadside to the sea. It began to roll.

Foster glanced at the body but the fishing basket seemed to be holding it.

He ran up fifty yards out from the surf, trying to spot the line of the sandbar. The tide was low and he didn't know the draught of the boat. If he tried to go across in too shallow water he'd run on to the bar. It was no use asking the dagoes what the boat drew.

The surf was fairly low but high enough to prevent his picking with certainty the line of the bar.

Foster stopped fifty yards out and watched the waves until a big one came along. Then he thrust the throttle forward and ran the boat in ahead of the wave. He felt the rudder kick as the crest caught the stern. He pushed the throttle full forward. He had underestimated the speed of the wave and the crest went past, letting the boat drop back. Foster brought the throttle right down, pushed the gear into reverse, then put the throttle forward, backing away from the surf.

Bill had gone straight in, confident in the familiar feel of the little boat and the knowledge that it only drew two feet.

Foster went in further ahead of the next big wave and caught it cleanly. The boat surged forward and Foster handled the wheel tenderly feeling the reaction of the rudder on the wave, keeping the bows at right angles to the sea so she wouldn't broach.

He could see the white glint of the sandbar in the clear shallow water behind the wave. The keel must have been nearly dragging the bottom. Then the wave broke on the other side of the bar and Foster turned the wheel hard over and headed upstream.

The green water of the river was running fast around the bend. Foster could see the people filing down the hill from the hotel behind the half dozen pines that lined the wide road along the river bank. He looked at the body outside the cabin. Salt had dried in white lines on the brown face. The eyes showed only the whites. The black, wet hair was spread down over the forehead.

Foster brought the boat into the wharf just as the first of the crowd arrived.

A strange, thin, sweet sound rose above the cry of seagulls, the swirl of water and the rattle of voices: Mad Mick was following the crowd down to the wharf, dancing in little shuffling steps, playing his flute. Mad Mick, who lived on the coins tossed to him by drinkers at the hotel and spent his days playing his flute and watching the queer world through the tangle of hair that fell over his mad eyes down to his twisted nose.

The two Italians became suddenly animated as Foster was tying the bow rope. They bolted out of the cabin and leaped on to the wharf. Then they seemed to sink into apathy again and stood by waiting for someone to do something.

The policeman, Rod Armstrong, jumped on to the boat as Foster was tying the stern rope. He knelt down by the body and inspected it briefly.

'He's dead enough,' he said to Foster.

'The poor bastard must have been under water for half an hour.'

'How'd it happen?' asked Armstrong, waving to a couple of ambulance men who were standing by with a stretcher. They carried the body to the ambulance.

'Not sure,' said Foster. 'He threw himself over with the anchor. He must have had the rope coiled and had his leg in the middle of the coil. I suppose the rope just tightened on his leg and pulled him over.'

'Couldn't they get him up?' said Armstrong.

'They couldn't pull a cork out of a bottle,' said Foster. 'Anyway, they panicked. It's a wonder they just didn't cut the rope and leave him there.'

'What did you do?' said Armstrong.

'Just pulled him up and tried mouth to mouth on him. Bloody awful. He hadn't shaved for a week.'

Armstrong looked over at the Italians who were now in the company of three or four of their countrymen and were explaining volubly what had happened. The townspeople crowded around them, listening blankly to the foreign language. They stared unashamedly, interested in the tragedy. Most of them were retired fishermen and any

15

news of the sea fascinated them. Foster glanced at the gaping, vacuous faces insensitively intruding into the grief of the Italians. Foster did no more than glance. He did not find their behaviour remarkable. They were behaving as he expected them to. They were his people.

'I suppose he did throw himself over,' said Armstrong. 'I mean they didn't tie the anchor around his leg and pitch it over themselves?'

'No,' said Foster. He didn't know why he was certain that hadn't happened but he was.

Foster looked for his own boat and saw it disappear around the second bend in the river. Bill was heading for their home wharf. He didn't like crowds.

"I'll come up and see you later,' said Armstrong. 'I'd better try and get some sense out of these dags.'

2

Armstrong came up to Foster's house late that after-noon. The two men sat on the small wooden verandah of the four-roomed fibro house, looking down across the river winding purple towards where the surf broke white over the bar on the edge of the darkening waters of the Pacific Ocean.

They drank beer while Armstrong made notes of Foster's account of the drowning.

'They'll want you at the Coroner's Court, you know,' said Armstrong when he'd finished.

'Yeah,' said Foster. He'd been a witness to the circum-stances of half a dozen drownings in his time and knew well the legal trappings that surrounded accidental death.

Armstrong neatly stowed his notebook in his breast pocket and buttoned the flap down.

'You know that's four dagoes been drowned down here in the last three years,' he said.

'Useless lot of buggers,' said Foster formally, ignoring the fact that probably four times as many white men had perished the same way in the same period.

'Of course,' said Armstrong pontifically, 'the trouble is they're only used to fishing in the Mediterranean—it's very different from here. You've never been over, have you, Jack?'

'No,' said Foster, picking up a bottle from the floor, and leaning over to fill Armstrong's glass.

'I went through it twice in the war and it's just like a great pond. You couldn't get into trouble on it if you tried. And then these silly buggers come out here and think they can sail on that.' Armstrong gestured at the darkening wastes of the sea stretching out to the horizon.

It occurred to neither man that the problems besetting a fisherman who tossed himself into the sea with an anchor rope round his leg were much the same in the Pacific as the Mediterranean.

'That's half the trouble with 'em fishing out the small stuff too,' said Armstrong. 'I've seen a hundred dagoes sitting on a wharf in Messina all catching sardines you wouldn't use for bait and catching 'em with great bloody rods, too.'

'Where's Messina?' said Foster.

'Sicily, little island off the bottom of Italy.' Armstrong's wartime travels had given him a much wider geographic knowledge than that normally possessed by the people of a south-coast fishing town. He knew that dagoes came from the northern side of the Mediterranean. The inhabitants of the other side were wogs.

'It amazes me that any of 'em ever fish in the open water,' continued Armstrong. 'They don't like it you know. That's why so many of 'em used to fish Sydney harbour. We had a lot of trouble with 'em. I was in the water police up there, you know.'

'Suppose they bloody near fished the place out,' said Foster.

'Fished it out?' said Armstrong. 'The bastards even cleaned up the jelly fish. Take out anything alive they would.' He thought for a moment then added inexplicably, 'And a lot that wasn't I daresay.'

Both men drank their beer in silence for a few moments.

'Actually,' said Armstrong, 'it's amazing what the bastards get away with. They used to net Middle Harbour, come down every night they would, and go through the place like a fine tooth comb.

'It was legal then and there was nothing we could do to stop 'em, but they were spoiling the fishing.

'Well, there was an old bloke used to live in a house down on the waterfront and he had a couple of traps and for years he'd been catching himself a few fish for his breakfast.

'Well, after these dagoes had been going through the place for a few months this old bloke—Charley Jones his name was—found he just wasn't getting any fish in his traps. Nothing in 'em at all—the dagoes were getting the lot.

'This stirked old Charley to death and he decided to fix the bastards, so he went up to the local tip and hauled back all the old iron and junk he could lay hands on and he sank all this stuff where the dagoes used to fish.

'Well, the next morning these dagoes come through—

19

two boats they had with the net between 'em like and starts to run over the ground.

'Naturally they hit old Charley's junk and rip the guts out of their nets. Must have cost 'em hundreds of quid.'

Foster laughed his approval and filled Armstrong's glass again.

'Yeah, but hang on,' said Armstrong. 'You haven't heard the rest of it yet. Old Charley was so happy at all this that he went down and told the dagoes that it served 'em right and that he'd put the junk there.

'Well, of course, it's against the law to drop scrap in the harbour and these dagoes went and reported him to us and old Charley was fined. It was me that had to hand him the summons.'

Foster laughed.

'Anyhow, that's dagoes for you,' said Armstrong. 'Incidentally, those two who had their brother drowned today want to sell their boat.'

'Why?' said Foster.

'Reckon they won't sail it again because it killed their brother.'

'Stupid bastards,' said Foster.

'They seem to expect me to sell it for them,' said Armstrong. 'Don't know why. They seem to expect you to do everything for them. Bloody good buy though; they only want three and a half thousand for it.'

'That is a bloody good buy,' said Foster. 'Why?'

'Don't know,' said Armstrong. 'I think they're really scared to get in it again. I reckon they want to be shot of it and get back to Italy.'

'God, I wouldn't mind buying it,' said Foster. 'A man could make a living out of a boat like that.'

'A man could make a hell of a good living out of a boat like that,' Foster told his wife over their evening meal.

His wife, a thin, dark wiry woman, moved across to the stove to pour boiling water from a kettle into the teapot.

'You'd never raise the money,' she said.

'I don't know,' said Foster. 'I might go and see Charlie about it tomorrow.'

'You're in to the neck to the bank already,' said his wife. 'Have you two done your homework?' she added to the two small boys who were mopping tomato sauce off their plates with bread and butter. She was assured that the homework had been done.

'Anyway,' she said, 'what would you want to go borrowing more to buy a boat for. You don't owe anything on the one you've got.'

'And I'm lucky if I make twenty-five quid a week out of it. If I had that dago's boat I could get in amongst the tuna. Bugger it, a man might make five thousand a season.'

'We're doing all right,' said the woman.

'We're doing all right!' said Foster. 'By the time I'm sixty I might own this box.' He gestured around the small kitchen. 'Big deal. If a bunch of useless bloody dagoes can own a boat like that why can't I?'

'Why don't you go look at television?' said his wife.

'I think I'll go for a bit of a walk.'

Foster walked down the hill from his house towards the main street of Bernadine. He walked past the little square timber and fibro houses, past the blue glow in the windows from the television screens.

In the still air he could hear the American accented dialogue in the inhuman familiar television tones. Most of the sets were tuned in to the same programme and the dialogue, receding and swelling as he walked past the houses, followed him down the street.

' *Do you mean you're going to have to operate, Doctor.*'

' *Yes, Mrs Vanders. But you mustn't be alarmed. An operation . . .*'

Foster walked unheeding. These were the night sounds of Bernadine, these and the steady black roar of the surf across the bar. The colours of the night were the black of the sky, the blue and red neon on Nick the Greek's cafe in the main street, the white blaze of the stars, the blue glow of television screens on the windows, the dark shadow of houses, the white blue of the road, the sand and the surf, the glaring shaft from the lighthouse three miles out to sea.

'*But Doctor, I'm frightened.*'

'*There's nothing to be frightened about, Mrs Vanders. Modern medicine . . .*'

The scream of a night bird, the drone of a car, Foster's muted footsteps on the sand-packed road.

He came to the house in which he had spent his childhood. A fibro box almost identical with the one he lived in now, almost identical with half the houses in the town.

Foster stopped. The house was in darkness except for a light in one of the back rooms. His mother had died in that house. Old Johnny Armstrong lived there now with his wife.

In the front of the house, behind the picket fence, was a bed of hydrangeas. Foster's mother had planted those. That was after his father had died.

Foster walked on towards the main street.

'*You know, Mrs Vanders, you can trust me. You believe that, don't you.*'

'*Yes, Doctor, somehow I think I do believe that.*'

3

'I'm not going out today,' said Foster. 'I'll drop the kids off at school.'

'What are you going to do?' asked his wife.

'Got a bit of business in town.'

'Are you still thinking about that boat?'

'Thinking about it, yes.'

'Well, don't do anything foolish.'

'I won't.'

Foster went out and started the engine of the Holden. He pressed the horn to sound a pomp tiddeley om pomp to bring the boys out. How the hell did Katey know he was going to look at that boat? Anyway there were no no fish around. He might as well have a day in town.

The boys came tumbling out of the house and scrambled into the back of the utility. Foster let in the clutch and drove off down the hill towards the school.

In any case the dagoes probably wouldn't sell for three and a half thousand. God, they'd get knocked down in the rush if they advertised it at that price. Armstrong probably had it wrong, or they would change their minds when they thought about it. It was worth going to have a look at it though.

The children got off at the school. Their faces took on the subdued different look they always had when they walked in the school gates.

' 'Bye, fellas. See you this afternoon.'

' 'Bye.'

Foster drove on down to his boat. Bill was on board working on the motor.

'We not going out today?' said Bill.

'You go out and see if you can get some flathead,' said Foster. 'I've got some business to do in town.'

'All right,' said Bill. 'We could do with a new set of spark plugs.'

'I'll get them,' said Foster.

'And it's payday.'

'I'll get that too,' said Foster.

He only paid the aborigine five pounds a week. That was why he had him as a sidekick. He couldn't have afforded to pay the standard rates. Bill slept on the boat and ate mostly fish so five pounds was all he needed. He preferred fishing to labouring or working in a factory.

Foster drove to the police station. It was only a wooden bungalow where Rod Armstrong lived.

'Rod,' said Foster. 'Are those dagoes off the boat still in town?'

'Yes, they're having the funeral the day after tomorrow. They're staying at the pub.'

'Are they there now?'

'Don't think so, they spent most of yesterday standing on the wharf looking at their precious boat. They're still trying to sell it. You thinking of buying it?'

'Wouldn't mind. You sure they said three and a half?'

'That's what they said.'

The Italians were sitting on the wharf with another man whose face was dark enough for Foster to class him as a dago.

The two brothers looked suspiciously at Foster, but nodded to him in recognition.

'G'day,' he said. 'They tell me you want to sell that boat.'

'Yes,' one of the Italians said. 'You like to buy it?'

'I might,' said Foster. 'Mind if I have a look?'

He went over the boat carefully and saw with distaste that the cut anchor rope was still lying in a pile where he had dropped it on the deck.

It was a good boat. Forty feet long, thirteen feet at the beam and probably drew about four and a half feet.

He pulled up the hatch cover on the stern and looked at the deep hold. It was already rigged for tuna bait. Along the back of the cabin was a rack holding tuna poles.

Foster went to the cabin and switched on the echo sounder. It was Japanese, he noted, still worth the better part of two hundred pounds.

Idly he turned the wheel, looked out through the windows at the broad strongly built bows. The boat would fish tuna now and this was September. Any day soon the

26

great shoals would come past. A lucky man could pull in five thousand pounds in a season.

Foster went back on to the wharf and looked down on the boat. A wooden plate screwed to the port bow bore the name *Santa Maria* in white paint. Awful bloody name for a boat, thought Foster.

'You got a Maritime Services Board Survey?' he said to the Italians.

They looked blankly at him.

'You know,' said Foster. 'Papers for the boat.'

One of the Italians pulled out a wallet, fished in it for a moment and handed Foster a Maritime Services Board Certificate declaring the boat to be in a seaworthy condition.

The Certificate was due to expire in another five months. There couldn't be much wrong with the boat. Nothing that a couple of hundred pounds wouldn't fix.

'How much do you want for it?' he asked.

'It's a very good boat,' said one of the Italians, the soft-looking one.

'How much do you want for it?'

'Thirty seven fifty,' said the Italian. 'That's very cheap; cost more than five thousand pounds.'

Foster looked at the boat.

'I might give you three thousand for it,' he said.

The Italian's voice rose to a higher pitch.

'No, no,' he said. 'It's a very good boat. Thirty seven fifty is very cheap.'

'Three thousand,' said Foster.

'I tell you,' said the Italian, 'I make a good price, thirty five hundred.'

'Look, do you want to sell the boat or not,' said Foster.

'We'll sell the boat,' said the Italian. 'But thirty five hundred is too cheap. A very good price.'

'I'll tell you what,' said Foster. 'I just might come to thirty two fifty. That's the end.'

The Italian's voice rose higher still.

'No,' he shouted. 'That's too little.'

'All right,' said Foster, 'shove it.' He turned away.

The Italian caught him before he reached his utility.

'You think about it and come back. Thirty five hundred is a very good price.'

'No,' said Foster.

'Thirty four hundred,' said the Italian, 'to make a bargain.'

'I'll come back and talk to you later,' said Foster. 'Will you be here all morning?'

'We will wait for you,' said the Italian.

Foster looked back at the boat as he drove off. Pity it had that dago name. He wouldn't change it either. It was bad luck to change the name of a boat. It would be a gift at four thousand. Surely the bank would lend him some money on a boat like that.

'Well, it's not really a banking proposition, Jack,' said the bank manager.

'Why not?' said Foster. 'I could probably pay the money back in a year.'

'I agree, you probably could,' said the bank manager. 'But it's not the sort of business the bank is looking for.' The pious phrases rolled glibly and effortlessly out of the man's thin, clerk's face. 'I could probably help you a bit.'

'How much?' said Foster.

'I don't know, we'll have a look at it in a moment. If we can help you get the deposit you can get the rest from a hire purchase company. Joe Lang would handle that for you. I'll give him a ring if you like.'

Foster waited while the bank manager dialled the number.

'Ah, Joe, Charlie here. Got a good client of ours wants to buy a boat. I was wondering could you help him? Jack Foster.

'He's got a chance of a good buy on that Italian boat. You know, the one that the fellow got drowned off yesterday . . . well, the purchase price would be about thirty five hundred, how much would he need?'

The bank manager picked up a pen and made notes on a pad on his desk.

'What would the rates be? And the terms? Insurance?

'Right, Joe, I'll see what we can do for him here then send him over to you.'

The bank manager turned back to Foster.

'Now, let's see what we can do for you. Joe says he could let you have a thousand. You could pay that over three years. Now, you've got a few hundred in the bank, haven't you?'

'I've got about seven hundred and fifty,' said Foster.

'And what do you owe on the house at the moment, do you know?'

'Fifteen hundred,' said Foster.

'It's worth about twenty seven and a half, isn't it?'

'About that.'

'Yes,' said the bank manager. 'Well, there's not much in that from the banking point of view. We don't like to lend more than half the value on a place, but I suppose, to stretch a point, we could give you say four hundred on that. That gives you eleven hundred and fifty. You're still over a thousand short, aren't you? It's going to be pretty hard, Jack.'

'I've got my own boat,' said Foster.

'Ah, yes, of course. Good. Well, there's about seven or eight hundred in that, isn't there?'

'I reckon,' said Foster.

'Well, we're nearly there. You'd be a bit short of ready cash. Why don't you go and see Joe and see if he'll stretch a point for you. He might come up five hundred'.

'I've got the utility too,' said Foster. 'Can't I borrow on that?'

'Well, not from the bank, Jack. You might be able to get Joe to give you a few quid on it.'

'It looks as though I might be able to drag it up one way or another, doesn't it?'

'You could,' said the bank manager cautiously. 'You'll be leaving yourself very short. It doesn't do to stretch yourself too much.'

'Well, how about lending me the money for a week or two so that I can do the deal with the dagoes and straighten it out afterwards.'

The bank manager laughed.

'God, Jack, you'd get me fired. That's not a banking proposition at all. I'll do what I can on second mortgage, but that's all I can promise. You'd have to do something about getting that down in six months, too. Go and have a yarn with Joe and see what he can do about dropping the deposit.'

'Not a chance,' said Joe. 'Absolutely dead against the

policy of the company. Sorry, Jack. I'd help you if I could.'

'All right, let's get it straight,' said Foster. 'If I put up two thousand four hundred you'll give me the rest, will you?'

'Sure,' said Joe. 'Assuming the boat stands up to valuation—and it would, I've seen it.'

'And how would I pay that back?'

'Over three years. The interest rate would be twelve per cent flat, so you'd pay it back at the rate of . . . let's see . . . thirty-seven pounds a month. You'd have the insurance on top of that. You'd have to insure it for what you owed us—a thousand. The insurance rates are four and a half per cent per annum on the amount insured so that would cost you forty-five quid a year. You'd be wise to insure for what you paid for it so it would cost you about a hundred and fifty a year.'

The figure rolled quickly and easily from Joe's genial fat lips.

'Have I got to pay that in cash too?' said Foster.

'No, we'd stretch a point and I think we could do something for you there, Jack.'

'What about the utility, would you lend me anything on that?'

'It's a Holden, isn't it? What year, Jack?'

'Fifty-four.'

'No, sorry, Jack, we're not lending on anything over ten years old at all.' Joe made it sound as though it were a matter of morals.

'So that's it,' said Foster. 'I put up twenty four hundred and I pay out something like fifty pounds a month for three years.'

31

'That's about it, Jack.'

'Not exactly marvellous bloody terms, are they?'

'That depends on how you look at it, Jack. Fishing boats are not particularly good business, are they? They generally get written off pretty fast. You've got to look at it this way: We lend you the money and it gives you the chance to get in amongst the tuna. I might lend you the money tomorrow and you might come in a week later and pay it all back. If you did do something like that you'd get a rebate on the interest.'

'All right,' said Foster. 'If I raise twenty-four hundred I can buy.'

'I'd say so, sure. You go and see what you can do about selling your own boat. I'll tell you who's looking for a boat at the moment—Dick Briggs. He'd be after something like yours. Let's see, it's about twelve o'clock now, he'd almost certain be down at the pub. Why don't you go and have a yarn with him? You can tell him we'll lend him half the money.'

'Why can you lend him half and not me?'

'A thousand's our limit at the moment, Jack; company policy—nothing to do with you.'

'I'll go see Dick and give you a ring.'

Briggs was in the bar of the hotel under the mounted head of the huge marlin a tourist had caught twenty years ago.

'G'day, Dick.'

'Jack.'

'How's the abalone going?'

Briggs was an abalone diver. He went out with a mate in a sixteen-foot boat with an outboard motor and dived for abalone in twenty feet of water whenever the sea was calm enough. The men shelled the abalone in between dives, then salted them and shipped them up to Sydney for canning. In a good day they might get forty pounds' worth between them, but good days weren't all that common.

'Getting a few,' said Briggs.

Foster ordered a beer.

'Just talking to Joe Lang. He said you're thinking about buying another boat.'

Foster sensed Briggs stiffening slightly.

'Thinking of it,' he said casually. 'Getting a bit tired of the diving. Wouldn't mind having a go at the fishing if I can get a decent boat cheap enough.'

'I'm selling mine,' said Foster. 'If I can get a reasonable price for it.'

'How much, Jack?'

'I reckon I'll get seven fifty for it.'

Briggs drained his beer glass. 'Another beer, Jack?'

'Thanks,' said Foster.

The barman pulled the beer.

'Not fishing today, Jack?' he said.

'No, got a bit of business in town.'

'Not many fish about anyway,' said the barman.

'I could be interested in your boat at seven fifty, Jack,' said Briggs. 'But I haven't got the cash. What would you say to four hundred down?'

'Joe reckons he'd lend you half. You wouldn't have to put that much down.'

'What boat are you buying?' said Briggs.

'Not sure, just looking around for something bigger.'

'They say that dago's boat's for sale.'

'Yeah, costs a lot of money though.'

Briggs stared thoughtfully at the wet patterns on the bar.

'You leave me the radio on your boat, Jack?'

'Yeah, as she stands. Take her over tomorrow if you want to.'

Briggs thought for a little longer.

"All right,' he said. 'You're on. It's a deal if Joe will give me the terms for half.'

They shook hands on it and Foster bought the other half of the round.

'Don't know anyone who wants to buy a utility, do you?'

'You moving out of town, Jack?'

'No, just reorganizing things a bit. What's the name of that car dealer at Yananbol?'

'Don't know, but I shouldn't think you'd get much of a price from a dealer.'

'No, I wouldn't buy it,' said the dealer. 'You can't shift that sort of stuff these days. I could give you a good price on a trade-in.'

'No, I want the cash,' said Foster.

'Well, I could do you terms. You'd get cash that way.'

'How do you mean?' said Foster.

'Well, we'll say you bought that Bedford over there. I could trade in yours at say three fifty, I could get you into the Bedford on a hundred pounds deposit and I'd give you two fifty in change.'

'How much do I pay off the Bedford then?' said Foster.

'I don't know, I'd have to work it out. Say about six quid a week.' The dealer shrugged off the matter of six pounds a week as being of no importance.

Foster went over the Bedford thoroughly. It wasn't any better than his own utility, although it was more than twice the price.

'Give us half an hour to think about it,' he said to the dealer. 'I'll come back.'

'Take all the time you want,' said the dealer.

Foster went into the usual Australian country town Greek café and uncritically ate the standard steak, greasy eggs and chips sluiced down with the uniform milky fluid the Greeks manage to produce under the general term coffee.

He worked his figures out with a stub of pencil on the border of a newspaper. He had seven hundred and fifty pounds in cash; he would get seven hundred and fifty pounds for his own boat. He was confident that deal would go through, he knew Briggs. Charlie at the bank would give him at least four hundred, that was nineteen hundred. If he did this deal on the Bedford he'd have another two hundred and fifty in cash, that was twenty one fifty. The dagoes might bring their price down a few more pounds or else he could probably screw it out of Charlie. He was being taken on the Bedford, but at least he gained cash.

That would leave him stark flat broke, with repayments of about eighteen pounds a week on the car and the boat. There was another four pounds a week on the house. He'd be cutting it bloody thin but the tuna season was just starting and there wasn't a boat on the coast that made less than three thousand pounds during the season.

Just one season like that and he'd be clear. He crumpled the newspaper and stared out through the café door to the car yard across the road. He could see the dealer, fat and affable, talking to a youth on a motor cycle. It would be better to wait and sell the car than go in for this deal, thought Foster. But if the dagoes were seriously trying to sell the boat it wouldn't last long at that price. Every fisherman on the coast wanted a boat like that. It meant big money when the tuna ran. Three or four thousand a year at least a man could make with a boat like that. He could build a decent house—the sort of house you saw in the city and the big towns—a house with three bedrooms and two living rooms, a room each for the boys. He had had a room to himself as a kid, but there'd only been him. His mother and father had used the other bedroom— until his father had gone. Foster grinned bitterly. What the hell was he always thinking about his father for lately. It was all bloody well tied up with money. Well, you didn't get money looking for flathead and schnapper.

Foster drained the milky dregs of his coffee, paid the bill and walked across to the car yard.

'You're on,' he said. 'Let's fill in the papers.'

He wanted to get back in time to see the Italians that afternoon.

There was a stranger with the Italians at the wharf. A man whom Foster would have distinguished by calling him 'a white man'. He was talking earnestly to the Italians and one of them broke away as Foster approached.

He smiled widely at Foster. 'You buy, eh?'

'I'll buy,' said Foster. 'Thirty-two fifty.'

'Ah,' said the Italian. 'We have a buyer for thirty-three hundred. We'll sell to you for thirty-four hundred.'

Foster looked across at the stranger. He looked like a

fisherman. The Italian's face was confident and Foster thought the other man probably was a buyer. If he was, if he had the money, if he had any sense at all, he'd go to thirty-four hundred.

Foster thought for a moment staring at the boat pulling at the bow rope in the running green stream. He already looked upon it as his boat. Who was this other bastard anyway? Caution tugged at Foster like temptation. But if he let this chance go he would wait another four years or more before he saved enough to buy a tuna boat. You just didn't get a tuna boat under five thousand. God, if he had the boat he could earn twelve thousand in those four years. But he was still two fifty short on the price. Bugger it, Charlie would come good with that. He'd have to. Or Foster could borrow it around town. He looked at the boat again. *Santa Maria*. Bloody awful name. But she was a nice boat. There couldn't be much wrong with it— nothing a couple of hundred couldn't fix. It was safe enough. The hire purchase was all right. Dick Briggs would pay all right. Foster looked once more at the *Santa Maria*, riding high by the wharf and was lost.

'All right,' he said flatly. 'I'll pay you thirty-four hundred. I'll give you twenty-four hundred now and the rest in a week's time.'

That would give him time to get the finance company's money through. If he couldn't get the extra money from the bank he'd get it somehow. Even if it meant selling the Bedford with whatever legal penalties that involved, he'd get the money.

'Is that a deal?' he said.

The Italian went over and talked to his brother excitedly in Italian.

The stranger drifted away to the end of the wharf looking at the boat.

The Italian came back.

'We fix this up with solicitor now?'

'If you like,' said Foster half contemptuous, half afraid of what he'd let himself in for.

Foster arranged to meet the Italians at the office of the solicitor they named in a town fifteen miles down the coast and went back to the bank manager to tell him what he had done.

'Well, you're putting me in a very difficult position, Jack,' said the bank manager. 'You're more or less forcing me into giving you the extra money, aren't you?'

'It's only two hundred and fifty quid extra,' said Foster. 'You said you'd give me four hundred.'

'But you're going to write a cheque now for two thousand four hundred pounds and you haven't even got the money for your own boat.'

'Joe said that could come through in a day. It should be here before this cheque appears.'

The bank manager looked worriedly at his desk.

'That means the bank will be holding six hundred and fifty as second mortgage on your home.'

'That's all right,' said Foster. 'I only owe fifteen hundred on it.'

'But that's not the point, Jack,' said the manager. 'It's just not sound banking to lend like that. The bank doesn't like it.'

What the hell was he carrying on about, thought Foster, it was nothing to a bank.

'I'll just give Joe a ring and make sure everything's straight his end.' And Foster knew all was well.

He waited stolidly while the bank manager phoned the finance company and learned in fact that the cheque for Foster's boat would be forthcoming and that the company was going to finance Foster into buying the Italians' boat.

'All right, Jack,' said the bank manager. 'I could get into trouble for this myself but I'll cover your cheque. I'll advance you the other two hundred and fifty you need to make it up, but you're cutting yourself very fine, Jack, and I'm going to tell you now it'll be no good coming to me for any more.'

'Thanks, Charlie,' said Foster. 'Do you know this solicitor character, Anderson, down at Landalar?'

'Yes, I know him quite well. He does a lot of work for the Italian community.'

'Is he all right?'

'Yes, very sound man I believe. You'll have nothing to worry about with him, Jack.'

The bank manager stood up with a rueful smile and shook hands.

'So, Jack, you've got your boat and I hope you do well with it. I suppose you're going straight down to the solicitor now, are you?'

'Well,' said the solicitor, tenderly patting the few hairs on his head. 'I take it what you're asking me to do is to prepare a terms contract. That means you,' he nodded at Foster, 'that means you sign a contract to the effect that you'll buy the boat and pay twenty-four hundred pounds now and you undertake to pay the balance in one week when your hire purchase finance goes through. That is the idea, isn't it?'

'Yes,' said Foster.

The solicitor leaned back in his chair.

'You understand, don't you, that under a terms contract, if you fail to meet the terms, the vendors, in this case our Italian friends here, can serve a summons on you to complete the contract. That is: pay the balance of the money, in this case one thousand pounds, or forfeit the money you've already paid. Do you understand that?'

'Yes,' said Foster.

'Might it not be wise to wait until the hire purchase money is actually available?'

'I don't mind,' said Foster. 'What about them?' He nodded at the two Italians sitting sombrely beside him.

'Excuse me,' said the solicitor. 'I'll just explain to them in their own language.' He spoke what sounded to Foster like fluent Italian and the two Italians spoke back to him with much excitement and moving of heads and arms.

'Well,' said the solicitor, 'our friends here say they have another buyer anxious to complete and they are not prepared to hold the transaction up—in other words they insist the contract is signed now or you must take your chances of the other buyer getting in first.'

The solicitor placed his hands on the desk and looked at them.

'That of course is not a very original statement from a vendor, Mr Foster. You must exercise your own judgement.'

Foster looked at him.

'I mean,' said the solicitor, 'that the pressure from another buyer may or may not be as great as suggested.'

'It doesn't matter,' said Foster. 'The money'll be through in a couple of days.'

'Then you want to sign now?' said the solicitor.

'That means the boat's mine then, doesn't it?'

'Yes. You take possession; and keep it, provided you pay the thousand in one week.'

'Then let's sign now.'

'If you'll wait in the outer office I'll get the girl to type out a contract and you can complete the transaction immediately.'

Within an hour Foster was the legal owner of the boat.

4

That afternoon the first of the tuna began to run. Only one boat struck them but it landed seven hundred pounds' worth of fish to the cannery. Foster saw the catch being unloaded as he drove the Bedford home.

He drove on down to his home wharf and found Bill just tying up.

'Where'd you get the ute, Jack?'

'Long story,' said Foster. 'Just take the *Elsie* round to the main wharf and unload all the gear into the dagoes' boat will you.'

'What?'

'You heard me, you black bastard,' said Foster jubilantly. 'We've got a real boat now.'

'Did you buy it?'

' 'Course I bought it. What did you think I did, steal

the bloody thing?'

'But where'd you get the money?'

'Ha, that'd be telling. Now get round there. And stay on board her and make sure those dagoes don't try to take anything off. She's all ours, son. All ours.'

Bill grinned.

'What's happening to the *Elsie*?'

'Dick Briggs bought her. Taking her over tomorrow. Leave all the fixed gear in her.'

'The clock and barometer and all?'

'Everything that's screwed on, son . . . just clear out the baskets and the lines and anything in the lockers.'

'O.K. Jack.'

Foster spun the Bedford around so that the wheels sent up a cloud of white dust and drove up the hill to his home.

'Where did you get that utility? Where's the Holden?'

'Long story, old girl,' said Foster, picking her up by her narrow waist and swinging her round the kitchen in a great circle to the imminent peril of the furniture and Katey.

'Don't, Jack. Don't be an idiot.'

'Hop in the car. I've got something to show you. Where's the kids?'

'Up the back. What have you done, Jack? Did you buy that boat?'

'Damn it all, Katey, what makes you think I'd do a thing like that?'

'Well, what have you done? You have bought it, haven't you?'

'Come and have a look.'

Foster pushed open the back door and bellowed: 'Hey you two. Come for a ride. I've got something to show you.'

'Hey Dad, is that your new ute outside?'

'Forget the ute. Just hop in the back. I've got something really good to show you.'

'Wait a minute, Jack. I've got the dinner in the oven.'

'Then turn it off,' roared Foster happily. 'Turn it off and come with me or I'll belt you on the bottom, you old scarecrow.'

'Don't drive so fast, Jack. Remember the boys are in the back.'

Foster obediently braked the utility back to thirty miles an hour.

As they came down to the wharf Katey said, 'There's Bill now. Did he get any flathead?'

'Flathead—who cares about flathead,' said Foster. He stopped the car and ran round to pull her out.

'Careful you lunatic. What's the matter with you anyway?'

The *Santa Maria* tugged gently at the ropes holding her to the wharf. Bill had Foster's old boat tied up alongside and he was throwing fishing baskets across to the *Santa Maria*.

'You did buy it,' said Katey. 'Oh Jack, should you have?'

The two boys hurtled along the wharf and on to the *Santa Maria*.

'Jack, where did you get the money?'

Foster thumped her thin little rump with the flat of his great hand.

'Do you like her, woman? Isn't she bloody marvellous?'

'She's got a funny name,' said Katey. 'But how did you buy it? Where did you get the money? And where did that utility come from? What's it all about?'

'Come and have a look at her, Katey. I'll explain it all to you after tea.'

'But you must be mad,' said Katey after tea. 'What are we going to live on?'

'You might have to scrape a bit, but look, this is September: The tuna are just starting. I've got right through to December. I tell you I'll pay off the hire purchase and the bank before Christmas—easily.'

'Maybe you will,' said Katey.

'Of course I will. God, you're a wet blanket of a woman.'

'Maybe I am. But . . . well, you know I didn't always see eye to eye with your mother . . . but I did agree with her about debts. She always used to say . . .'

'I know,' cut in Foster. ' "It was debts that ruined your father." '

'Your father, not mine,' said Katey. 'My father was never in debt in his life.'

'Leave it alone, will you, Katey,' said Foster, irritably. 'Leave it alone for God's sake.'

'It's all very well for you to shout,' said Katey, 'but you know how your father ended up. And you know what happened to your mother because of it.'

'What the hell's that got to do with anything,' said Foster.

'I don't like all this borrowing money.'

'No and I don't want to live in a box like this all my life and I don't want to end up on a pension and I don't want the kids to have to work for peanuts half their lives like I have.'

'There's nothing wrong with work,' said Katey primly.

'Oh for God's sake,' said Foster.

'If your father . . .'

'Shut up about my father, Katey.'

'All right, Jack, let's not fight,' said Katey.

'All right,' said Foster, 'let's not fight. I'm going out for a while.'

'Don't you come home stinking drunk.'

'I won't, I won't,' said Foster irritably.

Foster went to the hotel. There was nowhere else to go in Bernadine at night. Any of his friends who was quarrelling with his wife, or wanted to talk, or just wanted to drink, would be at the hotel.

He strode quickly down the hill towards the one street of shops that made up the centre of Bernadine.

Twenty or thirty cars were angle parked outside the hotel. Foster glanced at the cars and knew who was inside drinking. The five or six vehicles he didn't know would belong to tourists or travelling salesmen.

Foster walked up the steps into the hotel trying to recapture the mood of elation he'd known when he'd taken Katey down to see the boat. Damn all women. A man could do nothing right in a woman's eyes. Not if it was new. All they ever wanted was the same old rut. Katey was a good girl, but damn it why couldn't she have been a bit more excited about the boat?

Unadmitted in his mind was the knowledge that in the hotel would be men who wished they had done what he had done, who would congratulate him with envy on his deal, who would wish him well and think they meant it, ignoring their furtive hope that he had made a mistake.

There were half a dozen groups of men drinking in the bar.

'Hi, Jack, how's the big boat owner?'

Foster grinned at the man who had spoken and waved an arm generally at the men who turned and greeted him.

'How are you gonna get the smell of garlic out of that boat, Jack?'

'You won't be able to smell anything but fish on that boat, boy,' said Foster.

It did not surprise him that all the men knew about the boat. It would have surprised him more if they didn't. The birth of a child, a death, the purchase of a car, of a house—knowledge of all of these was the common property of the town; a buy like Foster's would naturally overshadow these more commonplace events.

Foster joined two men in overalls drinking under the mounted marlin's head above the bar. He grinned at the barmaid who was already pulling him a beer. No one asked him what he wanted to drink; everyone drank beer socially in Bernadine and even in winter they drank it so cold it ached in the throat. You might drink rum or brandy if you came in soaked from a gale with the bitter salt water leaking into your bones, but if you drank for pleasure you drank cold beer, if you were an Australian, a white man.

Foster's two drinking companions were both fishermen. One, Alec Normington, a tall heavily built man of fifty, owned his own tuna boat. The other, a short stumpy man of forty, was Bob Alton, who picked up a living working on other men's boats. Both were wearing black, heavy, turtle neck sweaters, and both had the leathery, lined, scaling faces and clear washed eyes of men who work in wind and weather and drink too much cold beer.

Alton pushed across some of the change he had lying on the bar to pay for Foster's beer.

'That sounds like a good buy of yours, Jack,' said Alton. 'Have you had her up yet?'

Foster drank half his beer and felt the cold thrust down his throat and spread around his stomach.

'She's going up tomorrow. Got to have her slipped for the survey—hire purchase, you know.' It wouldn't occur to him to conceal the details of his personal financial arrangements. It wouldn't have done any good anyway, everyone would know, somehow.

'And the dagoes wouldn't sail her because that bloke got drowned,' said Normington.

'That's what they say.'

'Sounds like a good sales line to me,' said Alton. 'Bet they drowned him themselves just so they could put that line across.'

'Or maybe Jack drowned him on purpose,' said Normington, 'just so he could get a good buy.'

All three men laughed. The death of an Italian wasn't a thing to be taken too seriously, or not talked about seriously. Foster half remembered the sharp stubble of beard cutting his own mouth, but you didn't think about things like that.

Foster bought a round of beer.

Normington ran his foot along the bar rail.

'You know why that rail's there?' he asked.

'To put your feet on,' said Foster.

'Well, that's what it's used for, but do you know why it was put there.'

'No,' said Foster amiably, waiting to be told. Most conversation in Bernadine was a series of statements of facts and counter facts, or narratives and counter narratives.

'Well,' said Normington, leaning on the bar, 'I don't know whether it's true or not, but the bloke that told me reckoned it was.

'Y'see, in the old days they used to take their drinking pretty seriously.' This statement, coming from a man who habitually drank a gallon of beer a day elicited no comment from his audience.

'And things were pretty tough. Well, it seems they didn't like to go out of the bar for a leak, or they didn't want to break off their drinking time. Anyway there used to be this trough running around the bar and the blokes would just stand there and leak into that.'

'Doesn't sound like the sort of drinking I'd like,' said Foster.

'No, but it just goes to show, doesn't it,' said Normington, running his foot reflectively along the brass rail.

Four Italians came into the bar and went down to the far corner by themselves away from the other drinkers. They were all big men and obviously fishermen. There was a stir in the bar as each of the groups of men turned to look at the newcomers.

'Better get out the vino, Mary,' somebody called to the barmaid. In fact the Italians, possibly to demonstrate that they had been assimilated, ordered beer.

'Look at 'em pretending they're men,' somebody said louder than was necessary. It was nine o'clock at night and most of the Australians in the bar had drunk half a gallon of beer apiece.

'Haven't seen those blokes before,' said Normington.

'There's a dago boat tied up at the bottom wharf,' said Alton. 'They're probably off that.'

'What sort of boat.'

'Tuna. Forty feet. Well rigged. Nice boat.'

'How do the bastards get boats like that,' said Normington. 'Half of 'em have only been in the country a couple of weeks. They can't even speak English most of 'em.'

The barmaid filled their glasses and Alton paid.

'I know how they do it,' he said. 'The bastards live on the smell of an oil rag. One of them comes out here, only costs 'em a tenner or something, and he takes two jobs in a factory, works night and day, eats nothing and in no time flat he's got the deposit on a house. Then he brings out ten of his mates and they all live in the house and they all have two jobs and next thing you know they've bought a boat or a taxi or what have you.'

'Bastards'll own the country before they're done,' said Normington.

Foster grunted assent. He wasn't particularly interested but it was normal to berate Italians in casual conversation.

'Of course,' said Alton knowledgeably, 'where they come from they never get anything to eat anyway and they're used to working all their lives. You and me couldn't do it. No white man could. It'd kill us.'

'They all carry knives too,' said Normington, 'cut your throat as soon as look at you.'

This was a little too much for even Foster's custom-blunted sense of justice.

'Come off it,' he said. 'I carry a knife most of the time, so do you. I bet you've got one on you now.' This was reasonably likely because Normington would have come straight to the hotel from the day's fishing.

'That's altogether different,' said Normington. 'It's a tool of me trade.'

'But bugger it,' said Foster, 'they're fishermen.'

'Yeah, but it's different. They carry 'em whether they're fishermen or not. They wear 'em to bed, they tell me.'

This, obscurely, prompted Alton to embark on lubricous tales of the sanitary customs in India, which he'd learned from a man who'd been to the place itself, and the evening wore on with tale and counter tale and round after round of ice cold beer.

Just before ten o'clock a man detached himself from a group at the far end of the bar and weaved solemnly through the smoke haze towards the toilets. He was a stranger to Foster, a short, sturdy little man of about thirty. He had red hair.

As he passed the Italians, who were still drinking quietly and talking among themselves, he stopped and peered at them. They ignored him, but a barely visible stiffening of their bodies showed they knew he was there. He stared soddenly at their backs for a moment, swaying gently backwards and forwards. The top of his head would barely have been on a level with the shoulders of the smallest of the Italians.

'That bloke's going to have a go at the dagoes,' said Alton.

'Silly sod,' said Foster.

The red head seemed to suddenly make up his mind, lurched forward and thrust his head between two of the Italians. His voice, harsh with the grinding, boring, pointless, vulgarity of his beer-soaked retarded mind, could be heard all through the bar.

'What you drinking there, eh? the old vino?'

The Italians crowded together to exclude him.

He clawed at the two nearest and thrust his way into the group.

'Hey, what is this? A man speaks to you civil and you push him out of the way. I asked you a question.'

The Italians looked down at him, unable to cope with the appalling piece of sodden ferocity in their midst.

'Well come on. I said what are you drinking—the old vino?'

One of the Italians said sullenly, 'We drink beer.' He gestured at the beer glasses on the bar.

'Oh,' said the red head, aping the gesture. 'We drinka da beer do we, we drinka da beer.' He turned to the rest of the bar at this and his freckled, cocky little face shone with the expectation of applause. He got none, but laughed heartily himself.

The Italians began to edge away from him, one reached for his beer.

'Hey hey,' said the red head, 'what's this? You sure that's beer?'

'It's beer,' said the Italian.

'It's a beer, is it? said the red head, 'but how do I know? How do I know you ain't fooling me? How do I know it's not some special sort of brown vino? Here, let me taste it.'

He lunged out and tried to grab the glass of beer from the Italian's hand. The Italian held on to it.

'Come on, let's have a taste,' said the red head and pulled violently at the glass. The Italian let go and the beer slopped down the red head's shirt.

'Why you dirty filthy dago bastard!'

The red head put the glass deliberately down on the bar.

'Right, now mop it up.'

The Italian looked at him woodenly.

'I said mop it up.'

The Italian turned to go away and the red head hit him savagely in the throat.

The Italian's three companions backed away and the Australians in the bar began to drift interestedly down towards the fracas.

The red head grabbed the Italian by the collar and tried to drag him forward. The Italian put up his hands and pushed at his assailant. The red head let go and stood back.

'So you wanta fight, eh? All right, come on then.' He adopted a boxing pose and the Italian waved his hands deprecatingly. The red head moved in and plunged his fists into the Italian's body.

Feebly, the Italian struck back and the blow caught the red head low on the body.

'You dirty dago bastard!' The little man, hard of body and anaesthetised by beer against fear, pain or pity, charged at the Italian with flailing arms and legs.

The Italian went down in an ungainly crumple with

the red head on top of him. Some of the men in the bar cheered. The Italian's companions looked on uncertainly.

'You'd think the bastards'd go and help their mate, wouldn't you,' said Normington contemptuously. Inasmuch as Foster ever made a moral judgement he recognised this as unfair. Had the Italians gone to the aid of their friend they would have been accused of ganging up on the Australian and an all-in brawl would most certainly have followed.

The red head was straddled across the Italian's chest punching him in the face. The Italian's nose was bleeding and splashes of blood spread over his face with every blow. He tried to push at the red head with his hands but he was barely conscious. The red head suddenly stopped punching him, grabbed him by the ears and began banging his head against the floor.

'That's about enough,' said Foster, 'he'll kill him.'

'Keep out of it,' said Normington.

'Bugger that, he'll kill him.' Foster put down his beer and walked down to the struggling men.

'All right mate, that'll do,' he said. The red head ignored him and kept banging the Italian's head on the floor. His hands were slippery with blood and he kept losing his hold on the man's ears so he wound his fingers in the thick lank hair instead.

'I said that'll do mate,' said Foster and shook the red head's shoulder.

The red head turned.

'Bugger off!' The words came from the animal lips in a little spurt of foam.

Foster bent down, grabbed the red head around the waist and lifted him clear into the air. The little man held on to the Italian's hair as long as he could and his hands finally came free grasping black tufts. He was struggling and kicking in Foster's arms. The Italian sat up with his forearms across his head to ward off further blows.

The red head seemed barely aware that Foster held him. He kicked out at the Italian, mouthing incoherent obscenities and clawing his hands at the air as though he was trying to break through some invisible barrier to get at his victim. It occurred to Foster that the man was genuinely a homicidal maniac, for the moment at least.

'Come on mate, calm down,' said Foster.

Another man, an Australian, a stranger to Foster, detached himself from the crowd which was now in a circle around the scene of action. He was a bigger man than Foster, a fisherman by the looks of him, and half drunk.

He grabbed Foster's shoulder with his left hand and cocked his right.

'Let me mate go,' he said simply.

Foster looked at the stranger calmly and clutched his arms tightly around the red head.

'I said let me mate go!' the cocked fist went back further.

'Don't be silly, mate,' said Foster, unworriedly. Foster knew himself to be in little danger. He was no Italian whose friends would weigh the consequences of helping him.

The stranger shook Foster's shoulder and Normington and two other men immediately moved in and grabbed his arms. He was hustled away to the other end of the bar and firmly told to behave himself.

The red head, aware now of something other than his

rage, had subsided. Foster put him down and pushed him gently away from the Italian.

'Go and have a drink and calm down,' said Foster.

The red head shook himself and then said aggrievedly, 'I was just going to have a leak.'

'Well go on then,' said Foster and the little man stolidly pursued the path he'd been on before he encountered the Italians.

The battered Italian had been helped to his feet and his friends were gently doing their best to mop him up.

'You bunch'd better push off before there's more trouble,' said Foster and the four men obediently shuffled out of the hotel.

Foster went back to his drink.

'You want to keep out of things like that,' said Normington sagely, 'you could get into a lot of trouble.'

'Couldn't let the bastard get killed,' said Foster.

Presently the little red head came back to the bar and weaved his way to his friend without so much as glancing at Foster or the blood that stained the floor.

'Good old Jack, the dagoes' friend,' someone called jovially.

It was meant in fun and Foster took it that way, but his grin was a little sheepish; it wasn't the sort of reputation a man wanted to get.

He finished his beer and announced that he was going home.

'Gonna try for the tuna tomorrow, Jack?' said Normington.

'No, got to slip her for the hire purchase.'

'That's right, you told me. See you, Jack.'

'See you.'

5

Foster eased the boat gently on to the cradle, then helped to set the arms to hold it.

Joe Taylor, the owner of the boatshed, had agreed to slip the boat on credit and also to supply Foster with enough diesel fuel to keep him at sea for a month.

The surveyor leaned on the wharf rail watching them. The arms were fixed and Foster started the electric winch. Slowly the cradle ran up the rails carrying the boat clear of the water.

Foster climbed off the slip and stood beside the surveyor.

'She hasn't been up for a long time, Jack,' said the surveyor, nodding at the streaming hull thickly studded with barnacle and weed.

'Dagoes had her,' said Foster.

'Copper sheathed,' said the surveyor. 'Have to take a bit of that off, Jack, to see what's underneath.'

'Ah, come off it,' said Foster. 'You hardly looked at my boat when you fixed it up for Dick Briggs.'

'Wasn't as much money involved there, Jack, and besides, I know your boat. Anyhow, look, there's a patch there I can get off easily. Only take half an hour.'

'What's it matter?' said Foster.

'Well, if you had a rotten keel and I let it go through and you wrecked the boat, the insurance company would still have to pay and I'd get sacked.'

'How the hell could the keel be rotten?'

'Anyhow, I've got to do it, Jack.'

Foster set about stripping the barnacle and weed from the boat. He would have liked to put a coat of anti-fouling on, but he didn't want to ask for more credit. It would do next time she came up.

The surveyor neatly removed the copper patch and began probing at the planking with a chisel.

'It looks pretty good, Jack,' he said.

'Well, there couldn't be much wrong with it,' said Foster.

The surveyor scratched at the exposed timber with the chisel.

'Few holes down here, could be cobra.'

'There wouldn't be many boats that didn't have a bit of cobra,' said Foster.

'No,' said the surveyor worriedly. 'There's quite a bit here, Jack.'

He was scraping away at the garboard planks, exposing several small holes about the size of a pin head.

'I'd better take a bit out,' he said.

He took a hammer and drove the chisel half an inch into the lower garboard plank just above the keel and gouged out a small block of wood. A black hole was exposed, as thick as a man's finger, running parallel with the planking.

'God, Jack, that's old,' said the surveyor.

Foster looked at the hole and thrust his finger into it. The cobra, the toredo worm, ate its way through the length of any boat, setting up rows of tunnels that left the exterior of the wood almost intact, but eventually made it so frail that it disintegrated under impact.

'It's probably down the keel too,' said the surveyor. 'I'll have to have a look.'

The cobra was right through the garboard planks on either side and through the keel itself.

'Blast it,' said Foster. But he wasn't unduly worried. The boat was seaworthy enough if he didn't hit a rock or another boat and he wouldn't do that. It'd only cost him a couple of hundred pounds to replace the keel and the planks eventually. The boat had been so cheap it would have been unreasonable not to expect to do some repairs.

'Bloody hard luck, Jack,' said the surveyor.

'It's not as bad as all that,' said Foster. 'I got the boat cheap enough. This will last through the season.'

'No, but you don't get my point, Jack. I can't give the boat a certificate.'

'What do you mean?' said Foster, and the surveyor sat up.

'I'm sorry, Jack, but I can't. It's not seaworthy.'

'Listen, matey,' said Foster very seriously. 'If you don't give me the survey certificate, how do I get the

59

finance on the boat?'

'It's not up to me, Jack,' said the surveyor. 'But I know no insurance company would insure it. You better go and see Joe Lang.'

'Yes, that's a bit of hard luck, Jack,' said Joe Lang. 'I can't give you the finance until I get that survey certificate, of course, but you go ahead and fix it and I'll put the finance through straight away as soon as I get the survey.'

'But damn it, Joe,' said Foster. 'You know I'm cleaned out now. I can't fix that keel until the end of the season. Even if I could, it would take a fortnight. You know I've got to pay off that boat in a week.'

'I know. I'm sorry, Jack, it's one of those things. Why don't you go and see Charlie at the bank, he'll probably see you through.'

'Absolutely no, Jack,' said Charlie. 'I've gone as far as I can go. It looks like I'm going to be in trouble now over you. I can't risk any more. You better try and get out of the deal.'

'But I don't want to get out of the deal,' said Foster. 'It's a good deal and this is all bloody nonsense and you know it. Just lend me the money to pay off the boat and a couple of hundred to fix the keel and it'll all go through in a couple of weeks, you know that.'

'Jack,' said the bank manager, 'you just don't understand. I can't put this through on my own authority. I'd have to ask permission through head office and frankly I wouldn't do it. It would just be a waste of time, and I couldn't recommend it to them. Go and see that solicitor again and tell him the deal's off.'

'Yes, well, I sympathise with your position, Mr Foster. I'll certainly ask our friends if they will cancel the deal, but you understand you have signed the contract. It's entirely in their power to force you to complete.'

'And if I can't?' said Foster.

'Well, Mr Foster, I went to some lengths to explain to you when you signed the contract that if you didn't complete you would be legally liable to forfeit the moneys you had already paid.'

'The lot?' said Foster, in whom a sullen anger was steadily rising.

'Well, yes, legally the lot. The vendors may see their way clear to refunding the moneys.' The solicitor paused and looked over Foster's head. 'Just as a side point. I wouldn't necessarily advise you to do anything drastic, but has the cheque been cleared?'

'Yes,' said Foster. 'They cashed it at my bank.'

'I see,' said the solicitor. 'Well, I'll ask them if they will cancel the deal. Perhaps if you'll give me a ring this afternoon.'

When Foster rang late that afternoon the solicitor said: 'I'm sorry, Mr Foster, the vendors are sticking by the letter of the agreement. I'm sorry about all this. I don't see that much can be done but perhaps you can consult another solicitor.'

'Never mind,' said Foster, 'just tell me what happens. So next Thursday I don't pay them, what happens then? Do they take the boat back?'

'No, the usual procedure is that they will issue a summons requiring you to complete, that is to pay the balance of the money, and if you don't do it within a fortnight from that date then they can re-possess the boat and retain the moneys paid. It's a rather harsh agreement but I'm afraid that's the law, Mr Foster.'

'Then I've got three weeks, is that right?' said Foster.

'Yes, that would be the position, Mr Foster.'

6

Foster drove down to the wharf where the *Santa Maria* was tied up. Bill was in the depths of the cabin working on the diesel. 'Looks like a damned good motor, Jack.'

'Hang around tonight, Bill. We'll go out after bait.'

'Tuna bait?'

'Yes, we'll go after the tuna tomorrow. I'll be down about eight o'clock tonight.'

'Right, Jack. Are you going to take a crew?'

'I'll go up to the pub and see if I can get one.'

A tuna crew would cost Foster no money. Men would work for eight pounds a ton shared between them, and the cannery would pay on delivery. But Foster had worked on the tuna boats for many seasons and knew that men would be hard to get now that the tuna were running.

There were fifteen or twenty men in the bar—there always were.

The slight pause before the drinkers greeted him told Foster they already knew about the cobra. They almost certainly knew the whole details of his financial predicament. It was said in Bernadine that no man could break wind without the whole town knowing it and it was said much more crudely than that.

Foster ordered a beer.

'Know anybody who'd want to come after tuna with me tomorrow?' he said to the bartender.

'I don't know, I'll ask around,' said the bartender.

This was the usual procedure. Anybody who now wanted to go fishing with Foster would approach him.

He drank two glasses of beer alone and knew that nobody would go fishing with him.

Instinctively he realized they thought his boat was unlucky and the term 'unlucky' had a peculiarly sinister connotation in Bernadine. They all knew the Italian had drowned on the boat. They all knew the boat had the cobra. They all knew that Foster was going to lose his money.

He had become involved in an unlucky boat. An unlucky boat would not get in among the tuna, that was the least that would happen to it. A man who went out on that boat would not get his eight pounds a ton.

There was no malice involved, but the tuna had started to run and any man who could hold a pole could get on a boat. They would have gone with Foster if there'd been nothing else offering, but there was plenty offering.

Foster drank his beer and went out to the street where it was growing dark.

The sea was dead calm that night and Foster ran the boat easily out over the bar, plunging irresistibly through the frail white line of foam that marked the crest of the feeble breakers.

He steered across to the island and dropped the stern anchor off a small inlet. He wished he had the bow anchor, now at the bottom of the sea on the other side of the island, but the water was calm and the one anchor would do.

Bill piled the bait net into the dinghy they had borrowed from the boat-shed and rowed out in a circle two hundred yards in perimeter from the boat, dropping the net out behind as he went.

Foster rigged a light on the boom, connected the generator and swung the boom out so the light hung fifteen feet from the boat. When Bill had half completed his circle Foster switched the light on, transfusing the black water with a green stain.

Soon a great brown cloud of yellow-tail flowed in from the blackness outside the circle of light and swarmed just below the surface of the water like moths gathering around a streetlight.

Bill came around rowing gently, made the complete circle and quickly pulled the net back into the dinghy until the circle shrank to a few square yards.

The brown cloud of fish swarmed densely in the light, crowding against the half inch mesh of the net and flooding into the centre of the circle, always drawn to the light, never diving below the edge of the net.

Bill and Foster took the long handled bait nets and stood side by side in the dinghy scooping the yellow-tail out in rapid sweeps and dumping them through the open hatch of the boat into the bait tank.

Again and again they drove the scoops into the living cloud of fish, taking out five pounds at a time and tossing them, flashing briefly silver, like a stream of illuminated hail, through the light of the lamp, into the darkness of the tank.

There were five hundred pounds of bait, thousands upon thousands of living fish, crammed into the bait tank before the two men stopped.

Still the brown cloud swarmed undiminished in the light. Bill pulled in the net while Foster swung the boom back and took the lamp off.

On the way back to the port Foster tuned the radio in to the weather forecasts and learned that tomorrow seas would be slight, winds moderate north to northeast—tuna weather, and cannery planes would be out spotting. Sixty boats would range over fifty miles of coast waiting for the tuna.

'Did you get a crew?' Bill said on the way back.

'No.'

'Going to make it hard to get a big catch,' said Bill.

Foster knew this but did not want to admit it to himself. Normally, in a boat this size, four men would fish for tuna while one stayed at the helm and kept the boat running with the fish. If he and Bill fished alone he would have to take the boat into the centre of the shoal and let it drift while they both fished. That meant they wouldn't have a great chance of getting many tons out before they lost the shoal.

A man might get in amongst the tuna five times in a season and each time he should win himself a thousand pounds worth of fish—if he had the crew to haul them in. But Foster stood one good chance: if he got into a shoal near one of the big cannery boats they'd give him crew.

Nobody would move into another man's shoal. The cannery boat would stand off until the small boat was full. The sooner it was full the more chance the cannery boat had of taking out a haul, so the skipper would lend men to the other boat.

The trouble with that, thought Foster, was that he didn't want to hang around a cannery boat waiting for the fish because the odds were that the cannery boat would get to the shoal before he did.

He would not let himself think about the odds in the enormous gamble to which he was committed, nor about the penalties of failure.

'But what's going to happen if you don't get any tuna?' said Katey.

'I'll get them.'

'But if you don't, you still owe the money to the bank, don't you?'

'Yes, I know that, but . . .'

'And you've still got the payments on that ridiculous Bedford?'

'I know all this, Katey—but one haul of tuna—one good haul and I'll get out of it.'

'One good haul in the next week.'

'I've got three weeks, Katey.'

'Three weeks!'

'Anyhow, for God's sake get off my back. I'll get the money.'

Later, while she was preparing for bed, Foster stood

behind her and put his hands on her thin shoulders.

'It'll be all right, Katey.'

She shrugged his hands off irritably.

'I want to go to sleep.'

In the familiar double bed they lay estranged. Foster moved restlessly for a few minutes, then his fisherman's mind, attuned to sleeping when it was time to sleep, began to slip away into vagueness.

In his half sleep, Foster suddenly started violently. His arm flung across Katey's body and Katey, who'd been waiting for him to say something, turned to him, and a little later Foster fell deeply and peacefully asleep.

7

At dawn he was out in the *Santa Maria* with Bill sitting beside him in the cabin, smoking. They swung past the pines, over the cool green running water, across the bar, through the gentle surf, out into the glittering silver sea with a white edged shoreline sliding away in a blue haze to the north and south.

The cannery plane was cruising up and down the coast in radio contact with all the boats waiting poised for a tuna run.

Bill let out three lines with feathered hooks to fish for striped tuna. These were only bait fish but every fisherman automatically trolled for them while he was at sea. The big eating tuna were the blue fin, the fierce fish that ran in shoals of millions from September to December—strong, sleek fish up to four feet long and forty pounds in weight—fish that brought tenpence a pound at the cannery—the blue fin tuna that every boat on the south coast was hunting today.

Foster gave the wheel to Bill, climbed up into the crow's-nest and stood there swaying in a gentle arc, searching for the ripple of tuna.

There wasn't another boat in sight which probably meant that most of them were much further out. That was any man's gamble. The tuna could come close to the shore or run twenty miles out where the continental shelf ended and the water went down two and a half thousand fathoms below the keel.

A dark wind ripple glided across the water a couple of hundred yards away. Foster glanced at it and rejected it. He could not have explained the difference in appearance between a wind ripple and a tuna ripple but he knew what it was.

A big bull seal came wallowing towards the boat. If he had been fishing Foster would have loaded the .303 he always took to sea and shot it. There was a strange truce between the fishermen and the seals. The fishermen left the seals alone if the boat were not actually fishing. If there were fish around the seals were ruthlessly despatched. A seal would send a school of fish diving deep or could tear a net to shreds in a matter of moments.

The cannery plane droned down from the north and passed slowly overhead.

Foster had been in the plane and knew that the pilot would spot any fish within twenty miles. The sea was a deep translucent map to the pilot and the fish would appear as thousands of distinct elongated grey ovals.

When he saw them the pilot would call their position

and the nearest boat would gain the haul.

Foster looked down to the stern and saw fish jumping on the troll lines. He swung down the rope ladder and swiftly hauled one line in, deftly coiling the thick cord on the deck and finally, with one long swing of the arm so the hook wouldn't loosen in its mouth, pulled a striped tuna from the foam above the screw and dropped it gasping on the deck.

Foster felt the other lines but there was nothing on them now.

The tuna's rigid body quivered and drummed violently, its gills gaping wide and black, its eyes rapidly glazing in the sun. Tuna don't live long out of water.

Foster dropped a gutting board—a sheet of three-ply—on the hatch cover, picked the tuna up by the natural handle of its rigid tail, laid it on the board and sliced two huge fillets off either side with a worn gutting knife honed to such sharpness that it slid effortlessly through the flesh. He cut the red meat into squares, then went into the cabin and looked at the thermometer.

All the tuna boats carry a thermometer rigged to gauge the temperature of the sea water. It was showing sixty-two degrees, which was good because the blue fin tuna only ran when the water temperature was between sixty and sixty-five degrees.

Foster looked at the echo sounder. The dark irregular shadow of the bottom was crowned with a fluctuating shadow that meant fish.

Probably rubbish, thought Foster. But he might pick up a few pounds with hand lines. There was no point in swinging on the crow's-nest all day. The cannery plane would see the tuna long before he did.

'We'll drift for a while and see what we can pick up,' he said to Bill.

Bill switched off the motor and went down to the stern to haul in the remaining troll lines. Then he and Foster baited the heavy gut hand lines with tuna flesh and tossed them over the side.

The boat drifted gently under the warm September sun. The two men put out the lines and felt them go slack as the lead reached the bottom.

Foster fitted a heavy rubber finger-stall over his index finger to protect it against the possible pull of a big fish which would drag the gut line in a burning streak deep into the flesh.

Bill didn't bother. His hands were calloused to the point where even a gutting knife would make little impression on them.

Foster could feel fish biting at the bait but it was only rubbish. He jerked the line savagely.

'Get away, you bastards.'

He pulled the line up, tore off the mangled bait, put on another square of tuna and dropped it over the side again.

A fierce double bite struck the line as soon as the lead hit the bottom.

Foster thrust forward his right hand, holding the line, waited for the instinctive moment, then ripped the line back and felt the sudden surging pull of the big fish. He hauled the line steadily and swiftly, keeping the pressure on the hook, gauging the weight of the fish and its type by the swerve on the line ten fathoms below.

'Schnapper,' he said. 'Big one. Get the gaff.'

Bill let go his line, took the gaff hook from the rack at the back of the cabin and leaned over the side.

The schnapper came up shearing sideways, broke the water in a flurry and Bill slammed the gaff hook into its head.

Foster kept the line taut as the fish came over the side and fell flopping on the deck.

Foster ripped out the hook, baited it and tossed it over into the water. Then he baited another four heavy gut lines and threw them over. This was early for schnapper and there wouldn't be many around but he'd get what he could.

Schnapper brought three shillings a pound off the wharf at Bernadine. A fish like the one gasping on the deck was worth thirty shillings. In season a man could catch thirty or forty like that in a day. He might be lucky today.

The big red-gold fish flapped ineffectually on the deck. The pale blue of the sky fitted like a saucer over the dark blue curve of the ocean. The two men sat and fished in the quiet and empty sea.

They pulled in a dozen schnapper in the next hour, but none as big as the first one.

If Foster had been working his old boat he would have been happy with a catch like this so early in the season, but now the money he needed was on a different scale.

A dark speck detached itself from the constant dark blur of the shoreline—another boat was heading towards them from the west.

'Who's that?' said Foster.

Bill stood up and peered at the approaching boat.

'Don't know,' he said. 'Probably comes from up north.'

The speck became the shape of a boat and then they

could see a man standing on the bows.

'He's looking at us,' said Bill. 'He's got glasses on us.'

Foster pulled another five-pound schnapper out of the water.

'How many men on board her?' he said.

'I can only see two,' said Bill.

The boat came briskly to within a hundred yards of where Foster and Bill were fishing.

'They're dagoes,' said Bill.

Dago was a general term covering anybody with swarthy skin.

The man with the binoculars had gone to the stern and was paying out a set line, perhaps a mile of cord supported in twenty-yard lengths by glass buoys with baited lines hanging between the buoys.

'He's seen the schnapper,' said Foster. 'The bastard could sit a bit further away.'

The strange boat kept moving in a semi-circle around Foster's boat with the line paying out as it went.

'Silly bastard, wasting his time with a set line,' said Foster. 'The small stuff'll chew off the bait before the schnapper get to it. What the hell is he doing?'

The strange boat was continuing its circle.

'He can't be going to go right around us. Not even a dago would be that mad.'

The strange boat kept on its course. Already the buoys were bobbing in a huge semi-circle.

Foster stood up.

'Watch what you're doing!' he roared.

The men on the other boat took no notice of him.

Foster stared at them unbelievingly. There was a certain ethic of the sea in this: if a man were catching fish you could come and fish near him provided you didn't interfere in any way. Running a set line around his boat came well within the category of interference.

The strange boat kept on its course until the circle was completed and a line of glass buoys lay on the surface of the sea completely enclosing Foster's boat.

It only meant that if Foster wanted to move he had to go across between the buoys where the weighted lines would hold the main line well down below the surface of the keel. But it was an unheard of thing for fishermen to do.

'Damn the bastard's rotten dago eyes,' said Foster. 'Pull in the lines.'

Foster and Bill quickly hauled up the lines and dropped them on the deck. Foster went into the cabin and started the motor.

'Just steer away from the dagoes and run along the buoys,' he said to Bill, then grabbed a gaff hook and leaped up to the bows.

The *Santa Maria* surged up to the line of buoys, then slowed down. Foster leaned far over the bows and smashed the nearest buoy with the gaff hook. The glass broke with a satisfying crash and vanished under the water. Bill steered alongside the line of buoys and Foster methodically smashed them one by one.

He could see the two Italians shaking their fists at him.

He smashed another half dozen of the buoys, then pulled up the next one with the gaff hook and slashed through the line with his gutting knife.

'Go back to the other end,' he shouted to Bill.

Bill swung the wheel over and drove the boat hard back across the remaining half circle of buoys.

Foster hooked up the first buoy they reached and cut the line again. Then as Bill, who knew exactly what was happening, steered up along the line again Foster leaned over and systematically smashed the rest of the buoys.

The last couple were dragged under by the weight of the line.

Half a mile or more of set line was sinking to the bottom of the sea.

'That'll teach the bastards,' said Foster.

The other boat was coming towards them now with a man standing in the bows carrying something in his hand.

Foster went down to the cabin, took the wheel from Bill and steered towards the other boat.

The man on the bows was a huge Italian about forty years old with the great rounded belly of a strong man. He held a bayonet in his right hand.

'What's he think he's going to do with that?' said Foster.

He stopped the motor and went up on to the bow.

'You dirty bastard,' screamed the Italian as his boat surged up.

'What do you want to do about it?' called Foster.

'I'll kill you,' screamed the Italian.

'Come on,' shouted Foster contemptuously.

'You sunk my line.'

'That's right. What the hell do you think you're doing dropping it around me like that?'

'I'll tell the police,' shouted the Italian.

'Do that—you fat gutted dago bastard.'

The Italian lapsed spluttering into his native tongue, turned to his companion in the cabin and screamed something at him. Immediately the Italian boat surged forward heading straight to hit Foster's boat amidships.

Foster leaped down to the cabin and started the motor. If the Italian hit him at any speed the heavy wooden bows would cut half-way through Foster's boat. Even a hard knock could spring the worm-eaten garboard planks.

Foster pushed the throttle forward and the Italian changed course to intercept him.

'I'll kill the bastard before he rams us!' Foster grabbed the .303 rifle from its case on the cabin floor.

He pulled a handful of cartridges from a box in the case and leaped down to the stern, knocking back the bolt and pushing a cartridge into the breach as he went.

The Italian boat was twenty yards off, bearing down fast on the *Santa Maria* with the fat man on the bows waving his bayonet and screaming.

Foster levelled the rifle.

'Stand off or I'll kill you!' he shouted, sighting at the fat gut that he couldn't miss even from the moving boat.

He could see the man's face clearly with its wild eyes and working mouth.

The boat came closer and Foster took up the slack on the trigger. It never occurred to him not to shoot, not to kill rather than let the Italian ram his boat. He wanted to send the bullet smashing through the great belly of the man shouting at him ten yards away.

Seagulls screamed excitedly above the water disturbed by the thrashing screws, unconcerned at the drama of the two men on little boats anxious to kill each other between the pale blue sky and the curved dark blue sea.

Foster thought he was quite calm, unaware of the lust for violence that gripped him. His finger began to tighten again on the trigger, taking up the fraction of an inch required to send the bullet tearing into the flesh of the Italian.

Ten feet off the Italian boat suddenly sheared and swung broadside to the *Santa Maria*.

Foster lowered the rifle and spat, laughing at the grimacing face of the Italian still screaming indistinctly on the bows.

Then on an impulse he raised the rifle and fired a shot over the man's head.

The Italians turned to the west and headed away from the *Santa Maria*.

'You should have shot him,' said Bill as Foster came back into the cabin.

'I bloody near did. Another two seconds and I would have killed him.'

Foster was surprised to find his whole body was shaking. His fingers could barely pull back the bolt to eject the spent cartridge.

'A man could get himself hanged like that,' he said aloud as he unloaded the rifle. 'I would have killed him.' He wondered at the ruin this would have brought him—ruin far more complete and final than the economic disaster he faced over the boat.

He looked at the rifle and then, not quite knowing why, flung it out through the cabin door and over the side of the boat. It went cleanly into the water with scarcely a splash.

'What did you do that for?' said Bill, startled for once.

'I don't want to kill any bastard,' said Foster roughly. 'Come on, let's get some schnapper.'

The day wore on and they pulled in a few more

schnapper and the cannery plane droned backwards and forwards through the clear sky.

No tuna were sighted.

Foster got twenty-five pounds for his schnapper at the wharf that evening. That didn't go far towards paying off the thousand on the boat.

8

'But how are you going to pay it off?' said Katey again. 'What's going to happen if you don't strike the tuna?'

'I'll get a job,' said Foster. 'I'll pull out of it and I'll get another boat.'

'And how long do you think it'll take you to do that.'

Foster didn't answer. It was a figure he wouldn't allow himself to work out. In any case, he didn't really look upon it as a possibility. There were only two things of importance that would really happen from now on. He would either strike the tuna or he would not. In either case he would reach an end of one sort or another.

'I'm going down to the pub for a while.'

'Yes, that'll help solve things, won't it?'

'I just might get someone to come out with me as crew,' said Foster mildly. But he knew he wouldn't. The cannery boats were advertising nine pounds a ton and they couldn't get all the men they wanted.

As he walked down to the hotel Foster noticed that the wind was rising. The usual dull roar of the surf was heightened tonight, vying even with the sounds from the television sets.

Bill was drinking in the bar with Dick Briggs and Foster joined them, feeling again the uneasy hush amongst the drinkers as they saw him. He accepted this. A man of misfortune aroused disquiet in those around him. That was the way things happened.

'How's the new boat going, Jack?' said Briggs.

'All right. Fine,' said Foster.

'Got some schnapper I hear.'

'A few,' said Foster.

'I got a few myself,' said Briggs. 'Fifteen quid's worth. I would have done better out of abalone today.'

'You'll do better later in the season,' said Foster.

'Yeah. You know they got a new lighthouse keeper on the Marabell Light?'

'Have they?' said Foster.

'A Canadian they say,' said Briggs. 'Funny bloke, they say he eats sultanas and oatmeal without milk or anything on it for breakfast.'

'Go on,' said Foster. 'I'm not surprised they go off their heads, living out there by themselves, with the bloody goats and the rabbits.'

Briggs stopped as though he'd remembered something. 'You know what they say a Marabell maiden is these days?'

'No,' said Foster.

'A goat that can run faster than a lighthouse keeper.'

Foster laughed before he saw the joke, then laughed again dutifully when he did see it.

The murmur of voices of the men in the bar rose and fell as constantly as the murmur of the surf on a quiet day.

Foster didn't bother to ask whether anyone wanted to join him as crew—he knew they'd approach him if they did.

Foster drank very slowly, making his beer last as long as he could.

'Hear about the dago and Gladys Williams?' said Bill.

'No—what?'

Briggs laughed: 'Haven't you heard that—funniest thing that's happened in town for years.'

'Well, what is it?'

'You tell him, Bill,' said Briggs—'I've got a bit to add to the end that'll kill you.'

Bill took a draught of beer and relit the handmade cigarette that hung from his lips.

'Well,' he said. 'You know Gladys walked out on her old man a year or so ago.'

'Mm,' said Foster. He wasn't interested in the gossip of the town, but it was something that happened—you had to hear it, a man who refused to listen to gossip would cut himself off from all human intercourse in Bernadine.

'Well,' said Bill, 'she's been letting a few of the blokes knock her off, you see . . ."

'Mm.'

'Well, this dago—Antonio or something his name is—is one of these blokes—he's knocked her off nice and regular.'

Briggs chuckled.

'Well,' said Bill, 'Gladys's old man gets to hear about

this—and he doesn't like it. It is bad enough the other blokes knocking her off—but when she takes on a dago, old Williams thinks it's a bit much.'

'Mm.'

'Well—Gladys is still living in their old house, you know, and her old man takes to hanging around outside waiting for this bloke to turn up.

'Well, the other night—the night before last it was—this Antonio turns up.

'He knocks on the door—Gladys opens it and in he goes—right as rain.

'Well, Gladys's old man waits for twenty minutes or so —reckoning that that'd be about the right time and then he charges in and he bangs on the door himself.'

Briggs began to thump his fist happily on the bar.

'Well,' said Bill, 'this frightens the life out of the dago and he takes off through the back window—with his trousers in his hand.

'Gladys's old man races round the back and catches him —giving him the father of a hiding and then goes off with his trousers.'

Bill and Briggs broke down and bent double with mirth. Foster laughed politely with them.

'They say, they say,' gasped Bill, 'they say the Eytie was walking down High Street without his trousers at three o'clock in the morning.'

'But hang on,' said Briggs, laying a hand on Foster's arm, 'wait till I tell you. I told my old woman about this and she said, " What a rotten thing to do." '

'And I said—"What do you mean? For the dago to be knocking off Gladys?" '

' "No," says my wife. "It was a rotten thing for

83

Gladys's old man to wait around until the poor fellow was shagged out and then beat him up." '

Briggs slapped the bar and roared with laughter.

' "Why couldn't he be a man," she said, "and beat him up before he went in and tired himself out." '

Foster and Bill joined companionably in the laughter.

'Mind you,' said Briggs, 'old Gladys must have slipped pretty low to take on an Eytie. They're all sex maniacs you know. I mean to say it stands to reason: they bring 'em out here without any women and they all live together. They tell me half these rapes you hear about are done by dagoes. I reckon a woman's pretty far gone to take on one.

'Still,' he added ruminatively, 'old Gladys is a bit of a bag; I suppose she's got to take what she can get.'

Foster finished his glass of beer.

'My round,' he said, sensitive to the idea that they might think he did not have enough money for drinks.

But he never bought the round because the door of the bar burst open and Armstrong, wearing his police uniform, came in.

He shouted authoritatively, 'There's a boat on the rocks at the bar, I want some men quickly.'

Immediately all the fishermen at the bar detached themselves from the drinking groups and moved towards the door. They drained their glasses as they went and left them on the ledge along the wall.

Briggs and Bill and Foster were the first and they piled into Armstrong's car. Two other men got in with them.

Armstrong drove off immediately, leaving the others to find their own way down to the bar.

'Who is it?' said Foster.

'Some bloke from Landalar. He stayed out too late and was trying to come in across the bar instead of going home. His motor cut out and he went on to the reef. He just called up on the radio.'

'How many on board?'

'Four,' said Armstrong. 'And two of them can't swim. It wouldn't do them much good anyway, they're two hundred yards out and it's a hell of a sea running.'

The police car stopped suddenly at the end of the road and the six men scrambled out and began running down the grassy bank towards the sand dunes.

There was a surf reel left permanently on both sides of the river at the entrance to the bar. Armstrong, although he was over forty, was a splendid swimmer and the men knew he expected them to pay out the line while he tried to swim out to the wrecked boat. They had all done it before. Foster, Bill and two other fishermen picked up the reel and began plodding across the sand towards the rocks. They could see a light flashing out in the dark seas beyond the foaming line of breakers. It seemed a long way off.

'You'll never get out there,' said Foster. 'You'll never get four of them in through that anyway. How about a boat?'

'Allan Purvis is trying to get a boat out,' said Armstrong. 'But he'll have a bloody full job getting across the bar tonight.'

Spray from the surf blew into the men's faces as they scrambled across the rocks towards the water. The wind seemed to be getting stronger. The night was quite clear but there was no moon. The sea was darkness with only the flickering distant light to show that there was life out there. Behind the men on the rocks the lights of the town glittered and away to the north the sands of the seashore were grey against the dull white line of the breakers, with the hills black against the night sky.

Foster could see the lights of a boat coming down the river.

'You'd better wait and see if Purvis gets out,' he said to Armstrong.

The boat was coming down fast. It swung around the bend and headed into the broken water behind the bar.

Foster knew that the men on board had no idea where the bar was at night. All they could do was wait until a big wave came through, then try to ride the backwash across the bar. The tide was high so they should be able to do it.

The six men on the rocks could see the boat as a dark shape on the driven white water. They saw the big wave —a high white crest rolling in it, saw the dark bows lift as the boat rose and went over.

Then the boat plunged forward through the surf, gathering speed as the backwash caught it and threw it towards the oncoming waves. The first wave broke just before the boat reached it and swung the bows hard round broadside to the sea.

'She's broached,' said someone on the rocks.

Unconsciously the hands of the men closed on imaginary wheels as they thought of what was happening in the cabin on the boat. The man at the helm had to get the bows around to the surf before the next wave came or the boat would roll over broadside.

'She won't get around,' someone said.

The next wave rolled over the boat, but by some trick

of wave and water she didn't turn.

On the rocks they could hear the motor racing as the helmsman tried to get the water-filled boat under way.

Another wave came racing across the bar and broke just behind the stern of the boat. All the helmsman could do was keep the throttle down and try to ride the wave. The boat rose and, with the bows thrust out before the wave, rode steady and straight towards the sand.

The wave was big, and took the shallow draught boat high up into the sloping sands before it dropped.

The men on the rocks sighed. The boat would be all right. It would sit there until morning, then they would drag it across to the river with a bulldozer.

If Purvis couldn't get across the bar nobody else would try.

'That's it,' said Armstrong. 'I guess I go for a swim.'

He stripped off his clothes and put on the canvas belt. He walked to the edge of the rocks gingerly because of the oysters, with the men taking positions to pay out the line behind him.

Armstrong waded into the shallow water off the end of the rocks, feeling the slight prickle of the kelp under his feet. The water was breaking on a minor reef further out and he had to get across that before he could swim. Foster and Bill followed him into the water holding the line high above their heads so it would stay clear of the rocks and the shallows.

Armstrong came to the reef, then plunged in and began swimming, diving under the waves. Foster lost sight of him and knew only by the steady pull on the rope that there was a man out there in the black water swimming towards the light.

Armstrong would have trouble keeping in a straight line because he wouldn't be able to see the light from among the waves.

At least there shouldn't be any sharks, thought Foster. There had been a time fifteen—twenty years before when he had seen a man go out on a line like this to a wrecked boat and suddenly the line had stopped pulling and all they had brought back to the beach was the head and shoulders of the swimmer.

The line was becoming heavy.

'It's picking up weed,' Foster shouted to Bill.

A swimmer didn't have much chance of getting out through the surf at night at best. He'd never make it if he were trying to pull half a ton of weed as well. The line became heavier and moved forward more slowly.

Foster could envisage Armstrong out there swimming hard against the sea, diving under the waves and struggling back to the surface with the growing weight of weed.

There was a sharp double pull on the line.

'Bring him back,' shouted Foster. 'He's had enough.'

They began to take up the slack on the line believing now that Armstrong was swimming back but then there was no slack, only heavy, dragging weight.

'I'll go out after him,' shouted Foster and began tearing off his clothes.

Then Armstrong appeared, standing up in the shallow water at the end of the reef.

'Not a chance,' he said when he reached Foster. 'I picked up a ton of weed. I had to let the line go.'

They stood looking out towards the light.

'Poor bastards,' said Armstrong. 'She must be breaking up.'

'Haven't they got a raft?' said Foster.

'Apparently not,' said Armstrong. 'They'll probably knock their roof off and try and float on that. They might have a chance like that.'

'They'd be halfway to New Zealand by tomorrow,' said Foster, 'if they stayed out all night in this sea.'

'The one that can swim might get in.'

'He'd have to be able to swim bloody well then,' said Foster.

The two men stood with the water swirling around their thighs, one naked and the other half naked, looking to sea, wondering whether death was happening out there.

'I might be able to get a dinghy out,' said Foster.

'What, over the bar? You're mad.'

'No, carry one across and throw it in here. I reckon it could be done.'

'Right,' said Armstrong. 'Let's have a go.'

They plunged out of the water and scrambled across the oyster-covered rocks.

Ten or so men were now hauling in the line.

'Half a dozen of you come with me and Jack,' said Armstrong, pulling on his trousers. 'We'll try and get a dinghy in.'

They drove to the boat-shed and got a twelve foot dinghy with a set of oars and an outboard motor. Someone had left a boat trailer at the shed. They commandeered this, lashed it to the bumper bar of the police car and dumped the boat on board it.

Four men stood on the trailer and held the boat in place as the car hauled it down to the sea.

They ran the trailer down over the sand and a few

yards across the rocks before it stuck. Then ten of them lifted the boat bodily and carried it.

'Who's coming?' said Armstrong when they reached the water's edge: 'You, Jack?'

'Bill and me'll do it,' said Foster.

Nobody argued this. Two men were the ideal crew for such a venture and they knew Foster and Bill were a team.

Bill sat in the stern and started the motor. Foster took the oars. Someone threw a bailing bucket into the boat. The other men held the boat steady until the screw bit and the boat moved forward through the water behind the minor reef.

Bill steered with the motor and Foster held the oars poised, ready to correct the course if the waves turned the bow. They went over the minor reef, through the rushing white water and they were in the surf.

The first wave came crashing down towards them, Foster dug the oars in and heaved forward with all the might of his back and shoulders. The bows crashed into the waves and went straight up so that Foster was looking down at Bill. For a moment the boat stood poised with its bow pointing directly at the stars, then it crashed over into the trough of the wave with the motor screaming even above the roar of the surf.

They made twenty feet before the next wave hit them. It was smaller and they went straight over it, but they took a lot of water on board.

'Bail!' shouted Foster.

Bill had already begun to scoop the water out with the bailing bucket. He couldn't get much out at a time because he had to control the outboard with one hand.

The boat was making little headway under the motor

and Foster heaved on the oars with maniacal energy, willing them not to break, willing the boat to go forward, to plunge into the wave already rolling down.

The boat lurched and he missed the water with one oar. The bows swung round to starboard and Foster dragged with all the strength of his back on the left-hand oar to bring the dinghy back head on to the waves. It almost came round but not quite.

The wave flung them high and foaming white water rolled over the stern. The motor cut out. The boat was half full of water.

'Bail, you black bastard,' screamed Foster hauling the dead weight of the boat through the sea towards the next wave.

Bill furiously scooped the water out of the boat and then, a fraction of a second before the next wave hit, slipped over the stern and used his body as a rudder to keep the bow to the sea.

The boat went straight up, water poured out of the stern over Bill's head as he hung there. He let go because his weight was dragging the stern down. For a moment he saw Foster lying back in the boat but still almost standing vertically. Then the boat was over the wave, crashing down into the trough. They were through the surf.

Bill was carried a few yards back but easily swam forward and climbed into the boat again.

It was half full of water and the bailing bucket was gone.

Foster rowed steadily out to sea over the rolling surf.

Bill took off his trousers, tied the legs in knots, filled them with the water inside the boat and began bailing.

Foster pulled towards the light on the water which he could see every time they rose to the top of the swell. There were more breakers out there where the sea struck the reef that had caught the wrecked boat.

The men would have to jump off the wreck and make their own way to the rescue boat. That was all right, the water should be shallow enough there. It depended on how bad the surf was.

Bill tried pulling the outboard motor over but it wouldn't fire.

The going was easier now because the boat was in a rip running away from the shore. But this would make it harder to get back with four more men on board.

Foster wished he had thought of taking the surf line out with him. With Bill holding it from the stern they probably would have kept it clear of the weed.

He could see the wreck every time he turned around now, a dark mass with one small light high on the mast, set on many acres of foaming white water.

The next time Foster looked the light wasn't there. The mast had probably come down. He could still see the shape of the boat against the foam, spread like a dull white stain on the black sea.

Foster stood off about twenty yards from the wreck. Every time he dropped into the swell he could see the cabin outlined against the sky. He couldn't tell whether there were any men on board or not. He didn't want to go any closer because of the broken water over the reef. The rip was pulling them further out to sea and he turned around and rowed against it.

'Ahoy!' he yelled. 'Can you hear me?'

But no answer came back over the sounds of wind and sea.

'They probably don't even know we're here.' Foster had to shout even to make Bill hear him. 'We'll have to go in.'

'I'll try and swim over to them if you like,' said Bill.

'Be buggered,' said Foster. 'You'd never find your way back. We'll go in to them.'

There was a fairly definite line to mark the edge of the reef. The waves were coming over from the east, breaking on the rocks around the stranded boat, swirling across the shallow water in a riot of foam, then fading in the heavy swell of the deep waters on the shore side of the reef before gathering momentum for the run on to the minor reef two hundred yards away.

The rowing boat began to dance when it hit the foaming water. Foster fought the waves and eddies to keep on course. Once they spun right round as a high roll of foam unexpectedly sheared up from the starboard.

They were within twenty feet of the boat and Bill saw a man standing on the cabin, silhouetted against the stars, waving something white.

It was all Foster could do to hold his bows to the sea. The broken waves would push them back, swinging the bows around and Foster would throw the whole strength of his body into hauling towards the wreck.

The water in the dinghy slopped backwards and forwards with every movement. Bill kept bailing with his trousers but wasn't getting much water out. The dinghy wouldn't sink with two of them on board. It would if it filled and they took on four other men.

Foster felt a sudden blow on one of the oars and then a heavy live weight. The dinghy swung around sideways to the foam and water poured in. Foster struggled with the oar, then realised there was a man hanging on to it. He let the dinghy go right round so that the stern was to the sea and hauled the man in by the oar.

The dinghy half filled as they dragged the man on board. He fell in a huddle between Foster and Bill. There was a line looped loosely around his waist. Foster ripped it free and flung himself into the bows of the dinghy, hauled in the line so that the dinghy swung round and pointed into the sea. The dinghy steadied but took on more water with every roll of foam that came by.

Foster held desperately on to the line. The other men would come down it from the stranded boat.

Foster ran the line through the ring-bolt and flung himself back to the oars. The boat was swinging around on the end of the line like a hooked shark.

Foster had to get the strain off the line or the weight of the man coming down it would pull the bows under. He bent his back to the oars and hauled the immense water-filled weight of the dinghy forward.

The weight of three men in the stern had the boat hopelessly out of trim. Foster let go of one oar for a moment, grabbed the huddled figure at his feet by the scruff of the neck and flung him bodily into the bows.

Another man appeared suddenly at the side of the boat. Foster hauled him in and again the dinghy was half full of water.

A third man caught at the port oar. Foster began to haul him in but suddenly the man let go and disappeared in the foam.

The fourth man came down the line and scrambled over the bows.

Foster leaned over backwards across the bodies of the two men in the bows and slipped the knot holding the line on the ring-bolt.

The dinghy swept back with the swirl of the foam, spinning around, taking on water.

They came out into the deep swell running swiftly with the rip because Foster didn't dare pull heavily for fear of sending the overloaded boat straight under.

Bill and one of the other men began bailing. Foster scanned the black waters for the man who'd disappeared into the foam. But there was no hope of finding him. Unless he was a crack swimmer the rip was carrying him far out into the Pacific Ocean by now.

Foster thought of simply running with the rip and drifting out to sea, counting on being found in the daylight, but the sea could rise further and the dinghy would not survive.

When the bailing had lowered the level of water in the dinghy by a few inches Foster began to pull steadily against the rip.

He could see the Marabell Light to starboard and the lights of the town to port. His best hope of getting ashore was to row up the coast and then try to ride the waves in across the bar.

For two hours in the darkness he pulled against the deep swell. He had to go half a mile past the bar because when he turned broadside to the rip it would carry him swiftly out to sea again. If he missed the bar the first time he would have to go right out and back again and he knew from the leaden pain that spread from his fingers through his whole body to his knees that he could not do it.

None of the men in the dinghy spoke. Bill and one of the survivors bailed steadily all the time. The man Foster had flung into the bows still lay there. The other survivor crouched in the bows holding his mate's head clear of the water that rolled backwards and forwards with every movement of the dinghy.

Foster could see lights moving on the beach and knew there were men there waiting, perhaps already expecting limp and sodden bodies to roll out of the surf like the debris of the sea. When the lights fell away behind him he knew he was far enough north. It was time to turn.

Foster swung broadside to the rip and pulled the dinghy swiftly down towards the surf. He could see the lights held by the men waiting on the sands going past as the rip pulled him southwards. It was as though he were stationary and the lights were moving north.

A wave gathered behind him and he bent his pain-wracked back to the oars and pulled and pulled as he thrust the dinghy on to the breaking crest, then felt the wave effortlessly take the weight and carry them in a roaring rush towards the shore.

The bows started to drop and Foster backed water, trying to hold back from the crest before it turned and smashed the boat upside-down on the five men it carried.

Bill flung himself over the stern and hung on, pulling the bows up and the dinghy stayed on the crest, careering across the bar with its human sea anchor trailing out behind.

Over the bar the wave broke and the swirl of foam carried the dinghy swiftly and gently on to the sand.

Bill waded out after it. Foster stepped into ankle deep water. Two of the survivors stood up, then collapsed into the arms of the men who came running up the beach. The third man didn't move from the bottom of the boat. He was dead.

9

The sea was still too rough for fishing on Saturday.

The *Santa Maria* stayed by the wharf fretting at her ropes as though anxious to slide out into the running green stream of water and down to the bar. Foster and Bill were working on the gear.

Two men walked down from the hotel, disturbing the seagulls feeding along the road. They came straight down to the wharf and stood looking at Foster and Bill for a moment.

'G'day,' said one eventually.

'G'day,' said Foster.

'We're looking for Jack Foster.'

'That's me,' said Foster.

'I'm Harry Yates,' said the man. 'This is John Denton.'

The man paused as though he expected some reaction.

'Yeah?' said Foster.

'We're the blokes you pulled out of the water last night,' said Yates.

'Oh,' Foster laughed. He jumped up on the wharf and shook hands. 'How are you?'

The men seemed embarrassed. 'We were wondering,' said Denton, 'you know, could we buy you a drink or something?'

'That's all right,' said Foster. 'I'll have a drink with you some time.'

Yates took out a packet of tobacco and rolled a cigarette. He offered the packet to Foster.

'Don't use them,' said Foster.

'Well, what we wanted to say,' said Yates, pausing to light a cigarette; 'It was—like—well thanks a lot for what you did.'

'Yeah, well that's all right,' said Foster laughing self-consciously.

He gestured with his thumb towards Bill who was working on the tuna poles.

'That's me mate Bill. He did most of the work you know.'

Yates and Denton gestured vaguely at Bill and said 'G'day.'

Bill gave them a brief nod.

'Who owned the boat?' said Foster, making conversation.

'John Brody,' said Yates. 'He was the bloke who didn't get into the dinghy.'

'They find him, do you know?' said Foster.

'No,' said Yates. 'That rip would have taken him right out to sea. He couldn't swim.'

'Who was the other bloke?'

'Bill they called him. We didn't know him. We only joined the boat yesterday.'

'How'd it happen?'

'Ah, Brody just tried to come in across the bar when the motor cut out. The rip carried us down and he hit that reef.'

'Why didn't you throw out an anchor?' said Foster.

'Didn't know the reef was there,' said Yates. 'Brody was trying to fix the motor and it looked as though we were just drifting down the coast. He was going to try and get into Mandolin instead. The sea wasn't too bad then you know. Then we hit the reef and couldn't get off.'

'Bad luck,' said Foster.

'Yeah.'

There was another pause. Yates's cigarette had begun to fall apart and he flicked the remains into the water.

'The copper was telling us you were looking for crew,' he said. 'We'll be in it if you like.'

'You fished tuna?' said Foster.

It didn't matter. Anybody could haul the fish out, but a man who knew how to do it wouldn't tire as quickly as a novice.

'Yeah,' said Yates. 'Five, six years.'

'Eight pounds a ton?' said Foster.

'Eight pounds a ton,' said the man.

'Six on the day and two at the end?'

This was the custom on the coast. The owners of the boats always held back some of the pay due to the men so they would stay throughout the season.

'That's O.K.' said Yates.

'Good,' said Foster. 'We'll go at five in the morning. The sea should be down by then.'

Foster took the *Santa Maria* ten miles off the coast on Sunday.

The sea was dead smooth, the water temperature sixty-three degrees. If ever the tuna were going to run they'd run today.

The cannery plane was out and every half hour or so they saw her fly across the sky from north to south, south to north.

Yates and Denton were lolling in the stern smoking. Bill was at the wheel. Foster was in the crow's-nest.

He could just see another boat on the horizon. A mutton bird, swift and brown, cut down from the sky, skimmed across the water and slipped away to the coast. Seagulls hovered around the stern, white and plump with mad, malevolent, red-rimmed eyes. One landed on the cabin and looked enquiringly at its own feet. Then, apparently alarmed at what it saw, fluttered off. The September sun beat warmly on the sea. The water to the east was a million acres of silver spangles.

The cannery plane came down from the north. Foster looked at it, then at the unmarked surface of the sea, then back to the plane.

The plane banked suddenly and slipped down towards the sea in a wide spiral.

Foster didn't realise what was happening for a moment. He'd visualised this too many times—the reality had the quality of illusion.

'Is the radio on, Bill?' he shouted.

'Yeah.'

The plane described two lazy circles, then the radio crackled into life.

'VHDJA, VHDJA calling. Who's that boat southwest of me now?'

Foster slid down one of the stays from the crow's-nest and snatched the radio mouthpiece from Bill's hands, at the same time he pushed the throttle forward and sent the boat at its full eight knots towards the circling plane.

'*Santa Maria*. Jack Foster. That you, Sid?'

'How are you, Jack? There's a patch of fish two miles northeast of you under where I'm circling.'

'Thanks, Sid,' said Foster. 'I'm on my way.'

'I'll stay over them until you see them.'

'Thanks, Sid.'

Foster handed the wheel to Bill and climbed back to the crow's-nest. He shielded his eyes against the glare of the glittering water, seeking the ripple that tuna would set up from three feet below the surface.

Yates and Denton took down their fishing poles and stood in the bows looking towards the plane.

'Hang a rack over the side,' called Foster. 'You two take the back. You stay at the wheel, Bill.'

Yates fixed the light wooden rack over the side for Foster to fish from. The rack was a small wooden frame that a man could stand in and hang over the water keeping both hands free to haul in the tuna. There was a permanent rack at the back of every tuna boat.

'You'd better put two out,' called Foster. 'We might have Bill fishing.'

Sometimes the tuna were not moving fast and it was not necessary to keep a man at the helm steering with them.

Yates and Denton fixed the racks, then lifted off the hatch cover and took down the bait nets.

Foster could see the other boat on the horizon steering towards them.

Fair enough, thought Foster, he would get there first. The other man could have anything he left over.

Yates and Denton checked the poles and squids—the feather lures with the heavy barbless hooks.

Foster saw the dark shadow on the water under the plane. A shadow like a breeze ruffling the surface but different.

'There's the rippler,' called Foster. 'Tell Sid I can see them.'

The plane waggled its wings then set off on its patrol to the south.

The ripple was moving very slowly, hardly travelling at all. That meant all four of them could fish.

Given two hours among the tuna, thought Foster, just two hours and he'd have the money. His whole being breathed out a plea to some undetermined and unthought of force to grant him just two hours among the fish.

Bill took the *Santa Maria* directly into the middle of the patch and cut the motor back to idle. As they crossed the edge of the shoal Yates and Denton began scooping the yellow-tail out of the hatch with the bait nets.

Foster dropped into the side rack.

The yellow-tail hit the water.

The whole sea around them suddenly seemed to disintegrate as ten thousand fish broke the surface and the tuna went streaking after the yellow-tail.

Foster flicked the lure down to the water and saw the fish he somehow knew would take it spurt up with gaping mouth. The mouth went over the lure and Foster swung the pole up, leading the fish along the line of its own impetus in an eight-foot arc to land on the deck.

The barbless hook slipped from the tuna's mouth. The line cracked as Foster slammed the hook back to the water straight into the mouth of the next striking tuna. He could hear the fish falling on the deck behind him as the other men hauled them in.

Foster fished so fast that one tuna would not hit the deck before the next was on its way out.

There was no great strength involved in pulling out the fish if you knew how to do it. Their own voracious speed took them out of the water into the air and the line and pole simply guided them round and on to the deck.

Bill was out fishing now because the school was not moving. The cracking of the lines merged into an almost continuous sound.

The warm-blooded tuna fell on to the deck and added the drumming of their dying bodies to the crack of the lines and the foaming hiss of the shoal devouring the yellow-tail.

A strange rhythm of sound: the slap of the fish on the deck, the crack of the lines, the hiss of the shoal, the drumming of the dying tuna.

In ten minutes there was a ton of tuna in the stern and the decks were already running with blood.

Somebody, Yates or Denton, threw another half dozen scoops of yellow-tail into the water and the surface boiled in new fury under the beating thrust of the frenzied fish.

Ten minutes more and another ton of tuna were drumming out their lives on the bodies of those already caught. A different sound now as the flailing tails hit tuna flesh instead of board.

The rest of the yellow-tail went over the side, and again the surface of the sea erupted in renewed fury.

Foster never took his eyes off the shoal, throwing the squid into the gaping mouths, flicking the vibrating fish on to the deck, cracking the line back to the water, one continuous circle of movement. With every swerve of his shoulder he landed forty pounds of tuna fish out of the sea.

An hour and a half more, another hour and a half, that was all he wanted.

The hiss of the tuna rose to a sudden fine crescendo and then they were gone.

Suddenly the surface of the sea was calm.

There was nothing there.

It happened between the time a fish fell from Foster's hook and the time his squid hit the water again. The mere cracking of the line and the squid fell into an empty sea.

Something had frightened them. Foster scrambled on to the deck, jammed his pole on to the rack, and climbed on to the crow's-nest.

'Start the motor,' he shouted to Bill as he stared around at the sea, seeking the dark moving patch.

God, they must be there. They had to be there. He had been too close. He couldn't miss now. There had been a thousand pounds' worth of tuna under his hands. He had to have them. God in Heaven, where were the tuna?

But the sun sparkled brightly on the sea and the gentle swell rolled eastwards smooth and blue, unmarred by the ripple of the shoal.

At sunset Foster brought the *Santa Maria* across the bar and the four men unloaded two and a half tons of tuna into the cannery truck. They picked them from the hatch and tossed them into the waiting truck. They took longer to unload them than they had taken to catch them.

But there were only two and a half tons. Two hundred and fifteen pounds in money, less the twenty quid he had to give to Yates and Denton.

It wasn't enough, not near enough.

10

'It's nowhere near enough,' Foster said to his wife, 'and great God Almighty, if I could have stayed among them for a couple of hours I'd have been right. I only need half a break.'

'Don't drink any more of that,' said Katey.

Foster slopped brandy into his glass and filled it with water from the tap over the sink.

'I'll be all right,' he said irritably.

'You're half stung now.'

'So what?'

'It's not going to do you any good.'

Foster drank half the glass in one gulp.

'You shouldn't have bought the boat, Jack.'

'What the bloody hell's the use of saying that now?' said Foster. 'I've bought it and I've got to pay for it.'

'All right, Jack, all right. I'm sorry. Could you sell the boat do you think?'

'I'm not going to sell it,' said Foster. 'I want that boat and I'm going to keep it.'

'I wish you wouldn't drink brandy, Jack,' said Katey. 'Go and buy some beer if you want to drink.'

'This'll do me,' said Foster, draining his glass and pouring more brandy into it. He didn't bother about the water this time.

'Please go to bed, Jack.'

'Oh, for God's sake leave me alone—I'm going out.'

Foster walked down to the town with the solemn intensity of drunkenness. He was aware of the wheeling brilliance of the stars and the diffused glow of the street-lights, of the houses and the row of shop fronts as the environment in which he moved. He was detached by alcohol from his normal involvement in matter.

The hotel was still open and automatically Foster walked towards the door. But then he stopped. Inside were men who knew of his troubles. If he went in he would be given a show of welcome: someone would drink with him, but he knew they would rather he was not there.

He knew the feeling himself. It was like if you met someone whose wife had just died, you spoke to them, sympathised with them, bought them a drink, but you were uncomfortable and you broke it off as soon as you decently could.

He turned and walked on down the street towards the wharves. The night was very still and clear. The slow roar of the surf struggled for a moment with the human sounds from the hotel, then won. The night smell of the sea beat images into Foster's fuddled brain and his walk took on the swaying deliberate movement of a man in a small boat.

The *Santa Maria* was tied up at the main wharf and Foster stood looking down at her. Dark and bulky, she moved on her mooring ropes with the downstream run of the current.

Foster remembered her as he'd first sighted her, tethered to the sea bottom with that fatal rope.

'I wish to God I'd never bloody well seen you,' he said aloud. But he didn't mean it. He wanted that boat with a passion akin to lust.

He stepped down heavily on to the foredeck. The *Santa Maria* jerked at her ropes and Foster stumbled.

'Bloody, rotten, stinking, worm-eaten dago tub,' he said, trying to evoke in himself a rage against the thing he loved.

He sat down on the hatch cover.

'A thousand bloody quid, a lousy thousand bloody quid.'

He leaned forward and ran his hands over the timbers of the deck. They were cold and wet with a light dew.

'This is my boat,' he said. 'This is my boat.' As though saying it would somehow dissipate the barrier of money that stood between him and total possession.

'Bugger it!' he said loudly and banged his fist on the hatch cover.

The door of the cabin opened and Bill came out. He looked forward and for a moment thought the massive shoulders above the hatch were part of the boat, so still they were. Then the fist beat down on the timber again.

'That you, Jack?' said Bill.

Foster turned slowly.

'Hi Bill,' he said.

'Hi Jack, what's wrong?'

'What's wrong? What the hell should be wrong? Bugger you for a start, you black bastard.'

Bill walked along the deck.

'What's up, Jack, you stung?'

'Stung? I'm pissed as a newt.'

'Like a drink?'

'Yes.'

'I got some rum.'

'I don't care what you got. Pour it out, mate, pour it out.'

Bill took out the enamel mugs they used for tea when they were at sea, half filled them with overproof rum, then filled them with water.

'Where's the bloody bottle, you lousy black bastard,' said Foster taking one of the mugs.

'In the cabin, Jack,' said Bill soothingly, unoffended by Foster's words. What a man actually said bore little resemblance to what he meant. Communication was on a different level from words. Bill knew that Foster's rage and insults were not directed at him, although he didn't even advert to the fact that he knew. This was just the way things were.

Foster drank his rum as though it was beer and Bill went back into the cabin and brought out the bottle and a saucepan full of water. He filled Foster's cup with the same mixture. It was not Bill's business to interfere if Foster wanted to drink himself blind.

'Life getting you down a bit, Jack?' he ventured.

'I'm all right,' said Foster, swigging the rum.

Both men sat silent in the darkness for a few moments.

'It doesn't matter, said Foster eventually.

'What doesn't matter, Jack?'

'Nothing bloody well matters. But it doesn't matter.'

Bill thought that over for a while.

'The dagoes getting you down, Jack?'

'Bugger the dagoes.'

'They're a dirty lot,' said Bill conventionally.

'Dagoes,' said Foster mildly. 'Dagoes. They're all right.'

'What? After what they done to you?'

Foster grinned into his rum.

'They didn't do anything to me, you stupid black bastard. I did it all myself.'

The clairvoyance of drunkenness lit Foster's brain. He was hardly aware that Bill was there. It wouldn't have mattered anyway: talking to Bill was like talking to a dog; you did it for your own sake rather than the dog's.

'A man always stuffs himself up. It runs in the family. My old man did.'

'Yeah, but Jack, those bloody dagoes . . .'

'Forget the bloody dagoes. It's just the way things are.' Foster thought about that for a moment, then said again, 'It's just the way things are.'

He drained his cup of rum and Bill refilled it. The world was beginning to slip away from Foster. He was meeting himself in the enclosing darkness of his own being.

'You do these things because you've got to,' he told himself, or Bill or whoever it was that was near him. He seemed to be near himself.

He shook his head.

'Mind you,' he said reasonably, 'I'm not buggered yet. Not yet. But it's hard to work out how I got here. You do these things because you've got to. No. That's not right. You do these things because there's nothing else you can do. You can't do anything else. That sounds the same, but it's different.'

He took another swig. Rum spilt on his legs and he brushed it away solemnly.

'It sounds the same, but it's different.'

Bill lit a cigarette and in the flare of the match saw Foster's sodden face with the half shut eyes staring out into the stream.

'It doesn't matter,' said Foster again. 'It's funny, but there's only a man himself. You get a wife and kids and a house and all that, but there's only yourself when it comes to the point. It's you that stuffs it all up.'

The cup of rum, forgotten, slipped from his fingers and clattered on to the deck. It occurred to Bill that if Foster didn't want the rum he might give it back, but he didn't say anything. Obviously Foster was unusually troubled about something, but if it wasn't because of those dagoes what was it all about?

'I wanted that boat, you know,' said Foster, as though he were somewhere else altogether. 'That was the trouble really. I wanted that boat. I wanted it because of the wife and kids.'

He sat up straight.

'No I bloody well didn't. I wanted it because I wanted it and I'm bloody well going to have it.'

Foster stood up and scrambled on to the wharf and stamped away up the hill towards his home. Bill looked after him wonderingly, then picked up the bottle, saucepan and cups and went back into the cabin.

Foster weaved his way home to a far from understanding Katey.

11

The clear September days rolled past and the tuna did not run.

A court officer served Foster with a summons requiring him to complete the transaction or surrender the boat and forfeit his deposit moneys. The man who served the summons was only a clerk but Foster was strongly tempted to pick him up and break his little body across the bows of the *Santa Maria*. But there was no point in that, so he just accepted the summons and the man grunted sympathetically and left him to it. Foster had two weeks left.

They were getting good catches to the south and Foster thought about going down there but he knew it was irrational. The tuna could rise anywhere over two hundred miles of coast. A man might sail a hundred miles today only to find they were making good catches at the place he had left. They were long quiet days from dawn to sunset, sailing ten, twenty, thirty miles out to sea and waiting, watching the cannery plane fly north and south, hauling in a few pounds' worth of schnapper, but mainly just waiting in the gentle swell.

One day they put out a set line but all they got was a white pointer shark. It came up tangled in half a mile of line. Foster hacked the shark to pieces as it lay alongside the *Santa Maria* to get the line clear.

As the mutilated body of the still-living shark sank they saw a boat with strange lines steaming across the horizon.

'That's a Jap,' said Yates.

'Too early,' said Foster.

The Japanese fishing boats put to sea for eight months at a time and usually around December they came to the New South Wales coast, fishing for the giant yellow fin tuna, six feet long and weighing eighty pounds. They caught them by letting out miles of set line and leaving it down for days at a time.

Many of the Australian fishing boats equipped themselves with set lines by waiting until they saw a Jap drop its line and sail over the horizon, then going out and stealing the lines.

'I know a bloke down at Malanda got almost two thousand pounds' worth of line from the Japs last season,' said Yates.

Foster watched the strange boat interestedly.

The line could be sold easily at half price. He didn't mind getting money that way.

The New South Wales fishermen were strictly honest

in their dealing amongst themselves but Japanese, in their eyes, had even less claim to human treatment than Italians.

But the strange ship went sailing on down the horizon and dropped no potentially valuable set lines.

In the town Foster found people withdrawing more and more from him. It wasn't that they disliked him, but they knew misfortune was closing on him and they felt uncomfortable in his presence. They felt as though they were in the company of a man suffering from a disease. They could do nothing about it, they couldn't help him, they'd sooner not know about it.

Even when Rod Armstrong came to tell him he was to be recommended for a medal for his rescue on the reef there was discomfort in Armstrong's speech, and he went away as soon as he could.

'A medal,' said Foster. 'A bloody medal. I need a medal don't I, like I need a hole in the head.'

Foster only saw the Italians who'd sold him the boat once in all this time. That was at the inquest on their brother. They looked very different sitting in the court in their stiff best suits.

The coroner delivered the inevitable finding of death through misadventure and Foster left the court with Armstrong. The Italians were met outside by half a dozen of their countrymen, all in their stiff best suits. They looked curiously at Foster as he walked past.

'I suppose they've never thanked you for what you did,' said Armstrong.

It had never occurred to Foster that he should be

thanked. He had done what he had done and that was it. Besides it was obvious to him that the thought uppermost in the Italians' minds was whether they would get their money. He was not the man who had tried to save their brother; he was a man who was in their debt.

'No,' he said.

The Italian group jammed itself into two cars and drove away.

'They changed their mind about going back to Italy quick enough.' said Armstrong.

'Yeah,' said Foster disinterestedly.

'They tell me the bastards have already bought another boat.'

'Is that so?'

'They're a funny lot.'

'Yes. They're a funny lot.'

On the nineteenth day after he bought the *Santa Maria* Foster brought her back to port after a fruitless day's searching and paid off Yates and Denton. He'd only had to give them twenty pounds between them.

'Sorry it's so light,' he said.

'That's all right, Jack,' said Yates.

'Pity we didn't get in amongst 'em,' said Denton.

Neither of the men was worried. They knew they'd have no trouble getting on another tuna boat, and they knew they'd strike the tuna sometime in the season.

'Yeah, well, we never did have that drink, Jack,' said Yates.

Foster understood this for what it was . . . an embarrassed allusion to the fact that both men owed him their lives.

'Yeah, we must do that sometime.'

'Yeah, well, so long, Jack, see you around.'

'See you around, Jack.'

'See you.'

The two men walked off up the white road to the hotel. They hadn't been surprised that they'd been paid off. They knew that this was the nineteenth day.

'Having a hard trot, that poor bastard,' said Yates.

'Yeah,' said Denton. 'Well, that's the way it goes.'

12

On the twentieth day after he bought the *Santa Maria*
Foster did not go to sea.

He got up late, drove the children to school, then came
back to the house.

His wife made no comment on his staying at home.
She had withdrawn into her own circle of worry and was
waiting dumbly for disaster to come about.

At half past nine Foster took the Bedford and drove
down the coast to see the solicitor who had handled the
purchase of the boat.

'I haven't been able to get the money,' he said. 'So
what now?'

The solicitor smoothed his hands over his almost hair-
less head.

'Well,' he said. 'Very much as I explained to you

before. As you know the time expires tomorrow and you are legally required to hand the vessel back to the vendors.'

'And what happens if I don't?' said Foster.

'I'm afraid you'd have to,' said the solicitor. 'The sheriff's officer would simply come and take possession of the boat. You would actually be holding it illegally unless you managed to obtain a court order staying execution, and I must say that my advice would be that no court would give such an order. It's very unfortunate.'

'And this happens tomorrow?' said Foster.

'Two weeks from the time the summons was issued, that's tomorrow isn't it?' said the solicitor.

'That's right,' said Foster. 'Then there's nothing I can do about this?'

'Nothing, I'm afraid,' said the solicitor. 'I did take it on myself to suggest to the vendors that they might care to be lenient under the circumstances, but I'm afraid they will not agree.'

'I've lost the lot?' said Foster. 'All the deposit?'

'That, I'm very much afraid, is the case,' said the solicitor.

'All right,' said Foster. 'Listen, I want some advice on another thing. I'll pay you for it.'

'Yes, go on, Mr Foster.'

'I've got a truck on hire purchase. I owe more money on it than it's worth. What happens if I give it back to the bloke that sold it to me?'

The solicitor gave a half smile. 'You do lead a complicated financial life for a fisherman Mr Foster.'

'Don't I,' said Foster.

'Well,' said the solicitor, leaning forward in his chair.

'In theory what happens is that the hire purchase company sells the vehicle at the market price and summonses you for the balance, if any, or refunds you anything the vehicle brings in excess of the money owing.'

'I see,' said Foster.

'But,' said the solicitor, 'that's the theory. If I were not speaking to you as a solicitor I might suggest that this very rarely happens. In fact, because the hire purchase companies do not like to draw attention to their practice of over-lending on vehicles, I have known it to happen that they issue the summons, but if Notice of Defence is lodged it's very rare for them to proceed to a court action.'

'I don't get it,' said Foster.

The solicitor leaned back in his chair. 'No,' he said. 'Well, to put it more bluntly, and I would like to make it clear that I'm not advising you as a solicitor, if you want to go back on a hire purchase deal just drop the vehicle back to the dealer. If you get a summons come and see me and we'll lodge a defence notice.'

'Good,' said Foster standing up. 'Thanks very much. There's one other thing.'

'Yes,' said the solicitor.

'Supposing, just supposing, I don't pay this money over tomorrow and they can't get their hands on the boat and then I finally turned up with the money. Do they have to take it?'

The solicitor laughed. 'That is a most improper question to ask a solicitor.'

'Yeah. Would they have to take it?'

'It's a nice point,' said the solicitor. 'I think I understand your meaning. I would not presume, of course, to attempt to understand your intention. Umm, put it this way. I would say that when the sheriff's officer finally caught up with a completely imaginary boat and the imaginary person in possession handed over a cheque on the spot, I would think that the sheriff's officer would accept the cheque and that any later court action would end in favour of the imaginary person in possession of the boat.'

'Again?' said Foster.

'I think it would be all right, son,' said the solicitor. 'But, I would deny ever having advised you to try a deal of this sort.'

Foster picked up two twenty-four gallon drums of diesel fuel and drove them down to the wharf.

'Lash these in the stern,' he told Bill, 'and hang around tonight. We'll be going after bait.'

'All right, Jack,' said Bill.

Foster called in on an insurance agent and took out a policy covering himself for five thousand pounds against death by accident in the next three months.

'That'll be right, Jack,' said the agent. 'I'll put it through.'

'I want to settle it now,' said Foster.

'I'll get out a cover note straight away and you'll get the bill in a week or so.'

'I want to settle it now,' said Foster.

'All right,' said the agent. 'If you want to. What's up? Do you think there's going to be an earthquake or something?'

'I just want to settle it,' said Foster.

'I'll just work out how much it costs.'

Foster drove to the bank and signed a cheque for one hundred pounds. The teller looked at it then muttered, 'I won't be a moment,' and disappeared into the rear of the office.

In a few moments the manager came out and beckoned Foster.

'Come in and sit down, Jack,' he said. 'I haven't seen you in a couple of weeks, how's it going?'

Foster could see his cheque on the manager's desk.

'You know bloody well how it's going,' he said.

'Yes, you've had a hard trot, Jack. I'm sorry about all this. What are you going to do?'

'I don't know,' said Foster.

The manager picked up the cheque. 'You know this cleans you out as far as the money you can take out goes.'

'I know,' said Foster, 'but I can take it out, can't I?'

'Well, yes, you can,' said the manager. 'But there's another payment due on the house next week.'

'I know that,' said Foster.

'And there's that second mortgage I gave you.'

'I've got a few months to do something about that, haven't I?' said Foster.

'Yes,' said the manager, 'but look, Jack, this is why I don't like these unusual banking propositions. I'm in a hell of a spot over this whole business.'

'What have you got to worry about?' said Foster.

'If you can't meet these payments the bank's got no alternative but to sell you out, you know, Jack.'

'Well,' said Foster.

'Well, I was just thinking,' said the manager, 'the way things are it mightn't be a bad idea to think about putting your house on the market. And do you think,' he looked at the cheque, 'do you think it's a good idea to go in for any more spending just now?'

'Look,' said Foster, 'are you going to cash that cheque or not?'

'But that's not the point at all, Jack,' said the manager. 'I have to cash this cheque, that's part of our agreement. The bank always stands by its agreement. I just thought it mightn't be a bad idea to have a little talk.'

'Just cash the cheque,' said Foster.

'If that's the way you want it,' said the manager, offended. 'But this is exactly the sort of situation we bankers are trying to avoid when we're not keen to lend money on propositions that aren't basically sound.'

'Just cash the cheque,' said Foster.

He spent five pounds on supplies of food and took them down to the boat.

'Stow that away,' he said to Bill. 'You got those drums lashed down yet?'

'Yes Jack,' said Bill. 'Going on a trip?'

'I'll let you know,' said Foster. 'I'll be back in a couple of hours, I've got to see a bloke up the coast.'

The dealer recognised Foster and greeted him with a hint of suspicion.

'Well, what can I do for you?'

'I brought your Bedford back. I don't want it,' said Foster.

The dealer looked at him sharply. 'What do you want me to do? Sell it for you?'

'I don't care what you do,' said Foster. 'I'm turning it in.'

'You're likely to find that a bit expensive,' said the dealer.

'Yeah? Well, here's the keys.'

'Listen, mate,' said the dealer, 'that's not my affair, this is between you and the hire purchase company.'

'Well, you tell them I've handed it back.'

'It's going to cost you a few quid. They'll just sell it at an auction. It won't bring much. You'll have to make up the difference between what it brings and what you owe.'

'Yeah, all right,' said Foster. 'We'll see.'

'Now listen, mate,' said the dealer. 'I did you a favour selling you that ute. You wanted cash and I gave it to you and put you into another vehicle. It's a pretty rotten thing to do just to dump it back here like that.'

'Do you want the keys or not?'

'I'm not going to take the keys,' said the dealer. 'It's got nothing to do with me.'

Foster threw the keys at his feet. 'See you later,' he said.

The dealer watched as Foster walked out of the yard into the street, then he bent down and picked up the keys. 'Bloody bastard,' he said viciously.

Foster hitched a lift back to Bernadine and walked up the hill to his home. His wife was in the kitchen.

'Listen, old girl,' he said. 'I'm going off tonight.'

'What do you mean?' she said sharply.

'Well, it's like this, if I'm here tomorrow they'll come and take the boat back. I'm done for then. I won't have a boat and I'm up to my ears to the bank. I'll be buggered.'

125

'Well?'

'Here's some dough,' said Foster. 'There's ninety quid there. Just pay anything you have to and hang on 'til I get back.'

'What are you goin' to do?' she said angrily because she was afraid.

'I'm going to stay out 'til I get the tuna. Now listen, I want you to do something. When I get a haul I'll radio Rod Armstrong to get in touch with you. I'm going to leave you a signed cheque for a thousand quid. When you get the message I want you to take this summons down to the Courthouse and hand it in with the cheque. But listen, and get this straight: I'm leaving the date off this. When you get the call fill the date in for the day after whatever it is. Do you get it?'

His wife was looking at him dumbly.

'Do you understand what I'm talking about,' he said harshly. 'Date the cheque the day after I call you, that'll give me a chance to get the money out of the cannery.'

'But where are you going?'

'I'm going to stay at sea until I get some fish,' said Foster.

'But it might be weeks.'

'So I'll stay at sea for weeks. I won't be able to put in anywhere in case they land on me so you won't hear from me, but don't worry.'

'Don't worry!' said his wife hysterically. 'What the hell do you think I am?'

'All right. Look, I'm sorry, old girl, but there's nothing else I can do.'

'Why don't you give the bloody boat back and stop all this nonsense.' Her voice had risen sharply.

'I'm not going to give that boat back,' said Foster flatly.

'But you can't stay at sea all the time. What about the weather?'

'I'll be all right,' said Foster. 'If it comes up bad I can get behind an island somewhere.'

His wife looked at him desperately.

'I'm sorry, old girl,' he said, 'but that's the way it's got to be. And listen, there's one other thing, don't take this too seriously, but—just in case—I took out an insurance policy. It's all fixed up. You'll get the papers in a few days. If anything should go wrong you'll get five thousand quid. That'll fix up the house and anything else and set you up for a bit.'

'God damn you, don't talk like that,' she screamed. 'Forget the whole bloody, stupid business. Give them back their wretched boat. You can get a job, we'll be all right.'

Tears were running out of her eyes. Foster hadn't seen his wife cry for ten years. Dimly he tried to allow his mind to tolerate the possibility of doing as she said, but a block of obstinate fear he could not recognise or understand stopped him.

'This is what I've got to do,' he said. 'It'll be all right, I'll get the fish and we'll be all right, you'll see. Now you understand that about the cheque.'

She turned suddenly back to the stove. 'I understand it,' she said.

'Now you won't hear anything from me at all. They'll probably try and call me on the radio, but I won't answer them in case someone comes out after me. I don't think they would, but I'm not going to answer anyway.

127

Now are you sure you understand that about the cheque?'

'I understand,' she said, her back towards him. She was doing something with a pan.

'All right,' said Foster. 'I'll be getting along then. I'll be seeing you.'

'Goodbye,' said his wife flatly.

Foster hesitated for a moment then turned and walked out.

She didn't turn round.

13

Foster walked down the sandy road to the wharf where the *Santa Maria* was tied up. It was late afternoon and the western sun was turning the further reaches of the river to purple and silver. The seagulls were feeding along the bank and flapping unconcernedly into the air as he walked past. It was very quiet apart from the screams of the gulls and Foster could hear the soft thump his booted feet made on the white road.

He walked on to the wharf and heard the sound of his footsteps change. Bill was sitting in the bow of the *Santa Maria*. He nodded as Foster came up.

Foster wasn't sure what to do about Bill. He needed him if he was to have anything like a reasonable chance of getting a pay haul of tuna. He thought about just putting to sea and taking Bill with him. But the black

129

bastard probably had a right to know what he was doing.

'Listen, Bill,' said Foster. 'You know I'm in a bit of trouble.'

This was the first time Foster's 'trouble' had been mentioned between them since the night Foster had been drunk.

'Yeah,' said Bill.

'I've got to pay out a lot of money on this boat tomorrow and I can't do-it. I'm going to put to sea and stay there until I get some tuna. Do you want to come?'

'Yeah,' said Bill.

'We might have to stay out a long time,' said Foster.

'Yeah,' said Bill.

Foster looked at the impassive black face sucking on the stub of a stained, hand-made cigarette. Then he shrugged and stepped on board the *Santa Maria*.

The tide was running out. Foster cast off the for'd rope. The bow of the *Santa Maria* swung out into the current. Foster went aft and cast off the stern rope. The boat drifted out into the middle of the stream.

Foster could see the drinkers on the hotel verandah up on the hill. They'd be watching him and wondering what he was doing. The insurance agent would have spread the story of the policy through the town by now. Probably the fact that he had taken the money out of the bank was widely known. They'd all be talking about it and wondering, although most of the fishermen would probably guess.

Foster turned the wheel to port and began running up the channel behind the surf. The *Santa Maria* was still in the calm water protected by the jagged rocks at the end of the spit.

The sea was flattened by the out-going tide and he had no trouble picking the sandbar. The boat began to rock in the broken water behind the bar and Foster turned to starboard, pushed the throttle forward and the *Santa Maria* sailed out over the Bernadine bar.

The town was behind them, its skyline darkly etched against the vivid orange flame of the western sky.

They'd still be watching from the pub, Foster thought, with their drinks in their hands, talking about him, debating his chances.

On impulse he turned the radio on. '. . . receiving me, Jack? Rod Armstrong calling *Santa Maria*. Are you receiving me, Jack? Rod Armstrong calling *Santa Maria*. Are you receiving me, Jack?'

'Yes, Rod,' said Foster.

'Where are you heading, mate?'

'Out to Marabell to get some bait,' said Foster.

'You haven't got a dinghy, Jack,' said Armstrong.

'That's right. Going to get them off the beach.'

'Hard way to do it, Jack.'

Foster didn't answer.

'When are you coming back, Jack?'

'When I've finished,' said Foster.

'Coming back tonight?' said Armstrong.

'It'll be hard luck if it takes me that long,' said Foster.

'Listen, Jack,' said Armstrong. Then he stopped. Foster knew that Armstrong was aware of the many receivers that would be tuned into their conversation. 'Give us a call when you're coming back, will you, Jack?'

'I'll do that,' said Foster. 'Over and out,' and he turned off the radio. He wondered whether Armstrong would be waiting on the wharf with the sheriff's officer and the

131

Italians when he finally did come back.

Foster took the *Santa Maria* into the one small bay on Marabell Island. It was a narrow bay flanked on both sides by rock and ending in a strip of white sand. There was a stone wharf near the mouth of the bay on the eastern side used for bringing supplies to the lighthouse. If the sea were running into the bay the waves crashed over the wharf and flooded across the sand to a barrier of broken rock, but in the calm weather the bay was dead flat.

Foster cut the motor and dropped out the stern anchor.

He took off his clothes, tied a line to the bait net, then dived into the water and swam the few yards to the shore trailing the line with him. He swam swiftly and thrashed his arms and legs furiously in case there was a shark lurking around the bay.

Standing on the rocks he pulled in the line and Bill fed the bait net over the bows. Foster walked around the edge of the bay hauling the net.

He swore as he cut his foot on an oyster and stopped for a moment to wash the cut in the sea water.

When he came to the sand he waded into the water to his waist, hauling with all his strength now because the net was getting heavy.

He came to the rocks again and pulled the net after him until he was abreast of the boat.

Bill hurled a coil of rope across to him. Foster tied one end of it to the net, then dropped a heavy rock on to the rope so the net wouldn't drift out into the bay. He dived into the water and swam swiftly back to the *Santa Maria* trailing the line behind him again.

The end of the bay was now almost encircled by the net leaving only a thirty-foot gap between the boat and the rocks on one side.

It was nearly dark now.

'We better have something to eat,' said Foster.

Bill put a kettle full of water on the butane cooker for tea. Foster opened a tin of camp pie and cut thick slices of bread. There was a grunting, screaming roar in the blackness of the rocks behind them and a heavy splash.

'Seal,' said Bill.

'Hope the bastard doesn't come in here,' said Foster.

If the seal came into the bay it could rip their net apart. Foster wished he had the .303. That had been a stupid bloody thing to do, he thought.

'Did you hear about the seal Charlie Blair shot?' said Bill.

'No. What?'

Bill laughed. 'His old man asked him to get him a seal skin 'cause he wanted to make a watchband out of it. Think of that, a whole bloody seal skin for a watchband! Anyhow, Charlie shot this seal one day and hauled it up in the boat and spent all the afternoon cutting the skin off it. Like skinning a bloody great cow it was.'

Foster spread butter on the bread, tipped the camp pie on to a sheet of newspaper and cut it in half.

'Anyhow,' said Bill. 'He gets his skin and someone told him you can cure it with tea you see, so he takes it out into his back yard and soaks it in tea.'

'Yeah?' said Foster, putting half of the camp pie between two slices of bread.

'Well, in about five days there was such a hell of a stink no one could get near his place and this hide's gone all green and slimey.'

Foster laughed. 'I'll bet.'

'Anyhow, Charlie's mate comes up and says the thing to do is to rub salt on it. So Charlie and his old man wrapped rags around their faces and spent another half day rubbing salt into this thing. The stink damn near killed them. They couldn't get it off themselves for days.'

'Yeah?'

'Anyhow, they went away and left the thing then. Just left it out in the sun. When they had a look at it again it was as hard as a rock. Just like one bloody great bit of board it was. Half as big as this boat.'

The kettle was boiling and Bill poured the water into the teapot. He sat down opposite Foster and put his half of the camp pie between two slices of bread.

'Anyhow, Charlie's old man never got his watchband. They couldn't cut the bloody skin with an axe. It's still up in his back yard.'

The two men ate their bread and camp pie and drank their tea, the light in the cabin a yellow square on the darkness of the bay.

Foster swung the boom out so the light shone on the water inside the almost complete circle of the net. At once a brown cloud of yellow-tail came swarming towards the light. Foster pulled at the line between the net and the shore so the rock was dislodged, then hauled the net in, completing the circle around the hordes of tiny fish. He began pulling the net on board and the circle closed tighter, compressing the frantic swarm.

Foster and Bill began scooping with the bait nets, tossing the tiny yellow-tail by the pound into the bait tanks. When the tank was full they swung the boom back, took down the light and hauled in the net.

Foster pulled up the stern anchor and set the *Santa Maria* for the open sea. He didn't want to be in sight of the shore by morning.

They dropped anchor for the night near the edge of the continental shelf and slept on the deck with the navigation light burning because they were on the coastal sea route.

Normally they would have made a bed from the bait net, but it was still wet and they lay on the bare boards of the stern deck.

It was a warm, still night and they lay uncovered, with blankets rolled under their heads.

Foster looked up at the stars, white and cold and remote flickering brilliantly in the black depths of the sky. The *Santa Maria* creaked gently and soberly as she rode at anchor in the calm sea. The fish in the bait tank splashed spasmodically. An infrequent wavelet slapped against the stern.

The salt smell of the wet bait net hung in the air, salt and the sharper tang of fish flesh. The timbers of the deck smelt softly of scrubbed wood and tar.

Foster turned and lay on his side, putting his face down close to the deck, closer to the clean wood. Think about Katey. She had a trick, when they were in bed, of running her hand. . . .

At dawn on the first day the thermometer showed the water temperature at fifty-seven degrees and Foster knew it would be no use climbing to the crow's-nest because the tuna never rose in water cooler than sixty degrees.

He pulled up the anchor and let the *Santa Maria* drift.

Bill threw a couple of lines over. He was fishing for food. The only commercial catch they could hope for was tuna. Anything else they caught would be spoiled before they put back to port.

Foster sat on the foredeck resting his back against the glass of the cabin window staring out at the brilliantly blue calm water. At nine o'clock the cannery plane came over for the first time and Foster switched on the radio.

'VHDJA, VHDJA. What boat is that northwest of me now?'

Foster considered not answering but he knew that the plane could easily come down and identify him. He picked up the radio mouthpiece.

'Jack Foster,' he said. 'That you Sid?'

'Oh, listen, Jack.' began the voice. 'They've been trying to . . .' Another voice cut across: 'Rod Armstrong, Jack, I was just about to send a general alarm out after you. Haven't you had your radio on?'

'No.'

'We were wondering why you didn't come back last night. Anything wrong?'

'No.'

'You coming back tonight?'

'Could be,' said Foster.

'All right, Jack,' said Armstrong. 'But you have to come back sometime you know.'

'I know,' said Foster.

There was a pause. Foster sensed again that Armstrong wanted to say more but was too aware of all the receivers that were listening.

'All right, Jack,' said Armstrong. 'Be seeing you.'

'Be seeing you,' said Foster. Then to the cannery plane:

'Any fish, Sid?'

'No, Jack, water's a bit cold in most places yet; might get better in an hour or two.'

The plane was almost out of sight now.

'See you, Sid.'

'See you, Jack.'

The pilot would know, too, thought Foster. Everybody would know. That night they'd be waiting on the pub verandah to see whether he'd come in. By now everybody would know about the food he'd bought. They'd be fairly certain what he was doing. He wondered whether the police would send a boat out after him. It didn't matter much because the only police boat on the coast was slower than the *Santa Maria*.

He turned the radio off. There was no hope of a call from the cannery plane while the water was cold. The morning sun grew hotter. Foster stripped off his shirt and sat down near Bill on one of the drums of diesel fuel lashed to the deck.

The boat moved rhythmically and slowly under the long, gentle swell of the sea. A seal broke the water twenty yards to the stern and turned its benevolent face towards them, then went about its business.

'It's a bull been kicked out on his own,' said Bill.

'Yeah?' said Foster.

'It's been cutting into somebody else's cows. Ever seen that, Jack?'

'No.'

'Funniest thing you ever saw,' said Bill clearing his line and re-baiting it. 'I was over on the island last year about this time and all these big old bulls were out there rolling around and gathering up all the cows they could.

137

Then one of the old bulls would try and get another one's cows and the two old fellows got stuck into each other, roaring and grunting and biting away.'

Bill dropped his line back into the water.

'Funniest thing you ever saw because all these young bulls are hanging around the edge, you see, and as soon as the old fellows get stuck into each other the young 'uns duck into the cows and root the arses off them.'

'Have seals got arses?' said Foster, laughing. Then, 'You ever married, Bill?' he said, unabashed by, in fact unaware of, the obvious chain of thought.

'I was once,' said Bill.

'Where is she now?' said Foster.

'Don't know,' said Bill. 'She only stayed with me a couple of weeks. She was a white woman, too.'

'God, when did this happen?'

'Five, six years ago. I was working on a station at Coolah. Got on the grog one night, met this woman at a pub and she came and shacked up with me.

'She stayed with me about a week and she was real good. Did the cooking and all, you know, looked after me clothes.

'Then suddenly she got it into her head she wanted to be married. Wouldn't have anything but I marry her.'

Bill paused and looked at the water in a puzzled fashion and laughed. 'So I married her, she fixed it all up. We went into town one day. Remember she made me shave real good for it and the fellow in the office married us all right.'

'Then we went back to the tent and everything was just all right for a couple more weeks, then she up and left me.

'Didn't say why, just got up one day, said she was going and went. Funny thing.'

Foster laughed. 'You could be worse off,' he said.

'I don't know,' said Bill. 'I didn't mind being married.'

'You might try it again sometime.'

'Not me,' said Bill. He laughed. 'Who'd want to marry a black bastard like me. Only a funny woman like that. It was good though. I was sorry when she went.'

A boat appeared as a black dot on the rim of the sea to the north. Foster watched it for a while, then started the motor and turned the *Santa Maria* towards the western horizon. He wanted to keep clear of other boats and it was just possible it might be the police.

Bill ran out a couple of tuna troll lines now that they were moving again.

Strange thing about Bill, thought Foster. He'd been with him for two years now and he'd never known anything about him before. What sort of a woman would it have been that would have married a black fellow. Not that there was anything wrong with Bill but you wouldn't expect a white woman to marry him.

Foster thought about his own wife. The kids would be at school by now and she'd be going around making the beds. How long had he been married? Eleven, no by God, twelve years. That was right, the oldest boy was ten now. What the hell was he going to do if this bloody business didn't work out right now? It would be rough on Katey, rougher than it would be on him, if they had to sell the house. God, but he'd been a fool to rush into the bloody boat. But then, curiously, he didn't really regret that. To have a boat like this was worth the risk—if it came off.

He wondered how Katey was feeling. She wouldn't

like being left alone at night. She always said the bed sloped the wrong way if his body wasn't in it and she couldn't go to sleep. It was really because she was a bit nervous about being alone in the night.

She was a good girl, Katey. He remembered when he had first met her thirteen, fourteen years ago. He'd been working on the cannery boat then. It was the end of the tuna season, after Christmas, and his pockets were full of money or it seemed a lot of money to him then. He was at the dance in the Soldiers' Memorial Hall. Who'd he been with? Could have been anybody in the town. All the men that he knew now had been there then except for the few that had drifted away and the few that drowned. He had seen Katey around the town before but hadn't taken much notice of her and then he saw her at this dance.

He'd been wearing a new suit and new shoes. He remembered the way his shoes had squeaked as he walked across the dance floor to ask Katey to dance. She'd been wearing a blue dress. He remembered that, or was it blue? It was a funny colour he remembered quite clearly but wasn't sure what name to give it. It was a sort of mixture. A bit like the colour of the water in the river just before the sun went down. Sort of blue and gold and purple. He had danced with her and they'd got talking and then somehow or other a few months later they'd got married.

Bill hauled in the tuna line and a striped tuna flopped gasping and drumming on the deck. Bill sliced off the thick fillets before the fish stopped quivering and brought them into the cabin.

'I'll cook these for dinner,' he said.

'Not for me you won't,' said Foster.

'Go on,' said Bill, 'they're good. Ever eaten them?'

'Yes, they're bloody awful.'

'You don't know how to cook them,' said Bill. 'You got to fry them in a lot of fat.'

'You cook them for yourself,' said Foster, 'I'll have the butcher's.' The butcher's was a golden, big-mouthed fish that Foster had caught early that morning. The name derived from its slippery skin which was supposed to be as greasy as a 'butcher's prick'.

Foster glanced at the thermometer. The reading was sixty-one degrees.

He looked around at the sea. There was no sign of the boat he had seen earlier. He cut the motor and climbed up into the crow's-nest. The sun was hot now and Foster shaded his eyes as he searched the slow, blue swell for the elusive ripple.

Bill pulled in the tuna lines and dropped a couple of weighted lines over the side, then sat down on the deck and began to smoke.

Foster wondered what his wife had told the kids about his absence. They'd be curious. He hadn't been away from home before for, God how long was it? He couldn't remember. A few years back he'd stayed out a couple of nights because the surf was bad. He had stayed in the lee of an island. That was about it.

It was hard to think now that at one stage he and Katey had thought they wouldn't have any children. They'd been married two years before she got pregnant. That was how he'd got his first boat. She'd kept working and they lived with his mother. They got together quite a few quid and they'd bought the boat outright. None of this bloody hire purchase nonsense for that boat.

They'd even picked up enough to get the deposit on the house. Katey didn't like living with his mother. It was a pity because the old lady had been renting the one house for fifteen years and the rent was dirt cheap. He and Katey could have stayed on until the old lady kicked off.

She'd been a tough old stick. When his father had died on her and left a ton of debts hanging around her neck she'd gone out and got a job in the cannery. Two pounds fifteen a week they'd paid her and she paid a pound a week off the debts and kept herself and him going for all those years.

God, but she had hated debts. She never put a thing on hire purchase. She'd even put threepences away to buy the old radio.

And when he was at school and big enough to get a few bob delivering papers and he'd wanted to buy a bike on hire purchase, she wouldn't let him. 'It was debts that ruined your father,' she used to say. That was all she ever did say about his father. Just that debts had ruined him.

So Foster had saved his money for the bike and by the time he had enough he didn't want a bike any more.

God, what would the old lady say if she could see him now? 'It was debts that ruined your father' probably.

Bill pulled a butcher's out of the quiet sea.

'I'll have that one,' called Foster. 'It'll be fresher. Use the other one for bait if you want to.'

'All right, Jack. Will I cook them now?'

'Might as well.'

Foster stayed in the crow's-nest and the crackle of the boiling fat mingled with the gentle creaking of the boat and the gentle slap of the water against the stern. The smell of frying fish rose to combat the clean tang of the salt sea that was so much a part of Foster's being that he never noticed it.

'Why don't you try a bit of this?' said Bill laying a great chunk of tuna on a slice of bread.

'I'll stick to the butcher's,' said Foster.

'Don't know what's good for you,' said Bill and sank his broken, stained teeth into the dripping mass of fish. 'It's not bad you know,' he said, chewing. 'A bit like schnapper.'

'I wouldn't be surprised,' said Foster.

The day drifted on and they saw no tuna and night came to turn the sea red, then green, then purple, then black.

The days went by, each almost exactly the same. Sometimes they saw a boat and steered away from it. The cannery plane was out every morning and every afternoon. The sea was calm. They ate fish and tinned meat and the last of their stale bread. They bathed in the sea very quickly, holding on to the stern rack because of possible sharks.

Foster spent most of the days in the crow's-nest.

Bill fished and smoked on the stern deck.

But never once did they see tuna.

A fatalistic tranquillity settled on Foster. It was not remarkable that they should sit so long without seeing fish. The tuna ran from September to December but a man might only see them and get in among them four or five times in these months. Foster knew he would strike them eventually. It was very rare for a tuna boat not to make a catch.

Only lack of fuel would send him back to port and his tank was still half full and he had the two drums lashed to the deck. He could stay out another month if he had to. He might have to pull into an island eventually to get water, but that would be all right.

14

On the seventh night out the two men were asleep on the stern deck on the beds they had fashioned from the bait net.

A cool touch of wind woke Foster and he sat up smelling the changed atmosphere of the night. It was very dark.

Foster stood up restlessly and looked around the deep black sea. There were no stars.

The western sky abruptly split apart as a great jagged line of lightning plunged down to the water. The crack of thunder came seconds later sounding like ten tons of coal dropped suddenly on to a metal plate. It was so dark Foster could not even see the bows of the boat.

Bill, awakened by the thunder, sat up.

'The weather report didn't say anything about a bloody storm,' he said.

Foster realised that the boat was beginning to rock. The wind was coming from the west. That was unusual at this time of year.

The lightning broke open the sky again, much closer this time and the thunder rolled over the sea.

'I'd better find out where we are,' said Foster, and clambered up to the crow's-nest in the darkness.

He could see nothing, only blackness, except for the tiny navigation light on the top of his own mast. The mast dipped in a long arc. The sea was coming up rapidly.

'I can't see any lights,' called Foster, but his voice was drowned in a roar of thunder.

He should be able to see lights somewhere along the coast. They couldn't have drifted far out to sea. There was probably heavy rain falling between him and the shore. He came down to the deck again.

'We'd better get behind one of the islands,' said Bill.

'Yes, but where are the bloody islands?' said Foster. 'It doesn't matter, we'll ride it out all right.'

The wind was blowing hard now and the rigging was whistling. The *Santa Maria* rolled heavily in a sideways swell.

Foster went to the cabin, started the motor and turned the bows around to the sea.

'You better get everything off the deck,' he said.

Bill cleared away the bait net and the fishing baskets.

Foster kept the throttle well back so there was just enough way on to keep the *Santa Maria*'s nose to the sea.

The lightning came more frequently with brighter flashes flooding with white light the rising water for miles around.

Foster looked at his watch. It was just on midnight.

Rain began to fall in a steady, drenching torrent, hissing into the sea.

The waves were coming towards them in great, long rolls, but they weren't breaking and the *Santa Maria* rose smoothly over them, her broad foredeck rising and falling well clear of the surface.

'I'll make some tea,' said Bill.

He put the kettle on the butane stove.

'Do you want anything to eat?'

'See if there's any biscuits left,' said Foster.

The bows were coming round in the sea and he gave the *Santa Maria* a little more power.

'You'd better try and fill the fuel tanks,' said Foster. 'We mightn't be able to do it later.'

Bill took a length of hose and went out on to the stern deck into the soaking rain. He unscrewed the cap on one of the diesel drums and thrust the hose in. He took off the hatch cover and unscrewed the cap from the fuel tank. He put one end of the hose in his mouth and sucked, breathing out through his nose so he could keep the vacuum in the hose. The diesel fuel came through·with a gush into his mouth. He spat and thrust the hose into the fuel tank. He kept his hand around the hose and the neck of the tank so that no rain would get into the fuel.

A bolt of lightning seemed to strike the sea twenty yards away. Involuntarily Bill clapped his hand across his eyes and the hose fell out of the drum on to the deck.

'Bugger it.' Bill put the hose back in the tank and sucked again. His mouth burned with the taste of the diesel.

The oil flowed into the fuel tank and Bill knelt on the

heaving deck until he had siphoned ten gallons out. He screwed the cap on the tank and came back into the cabin.

The *Santa Maria* rose mightily over the crest of a wave and plunged down the other side. The kettle fell off the butane stove and poured hot water over Bill's feet. He turned off the stove and put the kettle away.

Bill rolled himself a cigarette and stood beside Foster staring out through the rain-streaked windows. There was just blackness. Then the lightning and they could see the rain spearing towards them and the silver light-lined patterns of water on the glass, then it would be black again.

'Hold the wheel,' said Foster, 'I'll go up and have a look.'

He couldn't even see the crow's-nest fifteen feet above him as he began to climb the ladder. Then a white streak of lightning spread a momentary glow in the clouds and he saw the top of the mast silhouetted for a brief moment.

The *Santa Maria* went straight down the side of one wave and dug deep into the next.

Foster was lying almost flat on the ladder. As the bows came up he was flung back and had to cling with all his strength to stop himself being tossed into the water.

He reached the crow's-nest and wrapped his arms around the mast. The rain beat in his face and spray was coming off the top of the waves now, spreading over the *Santa Maria*, silver-filmed by the lightning.

The whole western sky burst into light and Foster thought he saw the dark mass of land, but it must have been cloud. There was no land out there, nothing that big anyway.

He tried to listen for the roar of breakers on the rocks of an island, but he could hear nothing except the sharp hiss of the rain, the loud rhythmical creaking of the *Santa Maria*, the howling of the wind and the broken rush of the water as the boat's bows hit the waves, all drowned by the crash of thunder whenever the lightning broke open the black sky.

Foster lowered himself to the deck. The bows went under and a couple of tons of water came over the decks tearing at Foster's legs. He waited until it was gone then wrenched open the door of the cabin and went in. He had to push hard to shut the door again. It was sticking. He didn't like that. The door of a cabin had to open easily because a man never knew when he might want to get out in a hurry.

'Where do you reckon we are, Jack?' said Bill.

'I don't know,' said Foster. 'I can't see a bloody thing out there. Have a look and see if she's taking in water.'

Bill took a torch and went down a short ladder from the cabin to the bilges. There was a little water down there, nothing to worry about.

Foster was thinking of the cobra-ridden garboard planks and keel. They'd be all right if he could keep the bows to the sea, but if the *Santa Maria* broached and the keel took the full force of water the garboard planks could spring.

He gave the engines a little more throttle. All the waves were breaking at the crests and the *Santa Maria* was either diving into the black troughs or soaring through the flurry of foam on their peaks.

The two men stood with their feet wide apart bending their legs to keep their bodies upright with each violent movement of the boat.

The lightning was so constant that for moments at a time they could see out across the wild waves, then complete blackness would envelop them to be split again a second later by the blinding sheets of white fire. They had to shout to make themselves heard.

Twice the bows went deeply under and the water crashed against the cabin. Both men knew that if once she went under too deeply and the water hit the glass it would come through and the cabin would fill with water. The *Santa Maria* might survive that once if the engines didn't go. She might even take it twice, but the third time would send her down into the forty fathoms of dark water below the keel.

'There's a light,' shouted Bill grabbing Foster's arm.

'Where?'

Bill pointed to the starboard. 'Over there,' he shouted. 'Behind us. She'll come around again in a minute.'

Then Foster saw it dimly through the pouring rain, the slow graceful sweep of a lighthouse beam.

A glare of lightning lit the sky and for a moment they both saw the whole island washed ghostly white in the glare, rimmed with a boiling circle of foam.

'We're past the bloody thing,' shouted Foster. 'It must be the Burlington Light. That's all it could be out here.'

They'd be sheltered in the water in the lee of the island, but if they went straight to it the *Santa Maria* would be broadside to the sea and Foster didn't think she'd take it. She was on full throttle now and barely making way.

Foster could go right round the island, coming into the lee, or could turn around now, run with the sea for a mile or so and come up into the lee that way. Either way it meant he had to come broadside to the sea sooner or later.

'We'll go around now,' he shouted and cut the motor right back.

The bows immediately swung round and the *Santa Maria* rolled deeply on her side in a trough. As she rose the water was pouring over her port rails. Foster thrust the throttle forward and turned the wheel hard over. The *Santa Maria* came around with ten tons of water on her stern deck and went soaring off down the wind.

She was running before the sea now and the waves were rolling forward with her, working on the rudder. The danger was that she'd go down in a trough and the following wave would fall on her.

A boat could go like that in a split second: one moment riding high and well and the next just gone.

They went down wind for a half a mile, then as a wave came past Foster pushed the throttle forward. The crest went under the *Santa Maria* and Foster spun her hard around and set a course diagonally across the run of the sea to the lee of the island.

The boat went half-broadside on into the next wave. She went under heavily on the port side then broke free, danced violently on the crest again and dropped with a heavy crash into the next trough.

'Bugger that,' said Foster. 'She'll tear her keel off.'

He swung her nose around to the sea again. Half a dozen jagged bursts of lightning broke at once. They saw the island again through the silvered rain. Multiple bursts of thunder drowned all other sound.

For a moment they seemed to pause, raised high on the waves, the sky a blaze of silver fire, the island ghostly

151

white with the lighthouse rising like a white finger, its light extinguished by the brilliance of the sky.

Like molten silver the water hung suspended on the windshield glass. There was a strange illusion of stillness and isolation in the cabin; a motionless point in the black, white and silver chaos of the night.

Then the moment passed and the *Santa Maria* plunged into the next black trough.

Foster kept the throttle down, letting the *Santa Maria* go backwards as wind and waves pushed at her. The bows started to come around and he gave her more throttle. He was letting the elements take her down across the sea as near as they would to the lee of the island. Then he would turn and make a run for the lee, hoping that the keel would stay on the hull.

The bows came around too much for a moment and she almost broached. Foster pushed the throttle full forward and turned the wheel over. The *Santa Maria* lurched around under full power from the screw and went straight down into the trough of a wave. The bows bit deep into the side of the next wave and tons of water came crashing on to the foredeck. As the bows came up the water pressed directly on the glass of the cabin. To the men inside it was as though they were actually beneath the sea. The glass bulged visibly, then burst with a loud mean crack and the water surged through the cabin, knocking Bill to the deck.

Foster held the wheel, pressing his body against the thrusts of the water. As the bows finally came out he swung the *Santa Maria* broadside to the sea. The diesel motor still thudded reassuringly but there was at least a ton of water in the bilges.

'Get on the pump!' Foster shouted.

Bill thrust the hose of the rotary pump through the shattered glass and began turning the handle.

The *Santa Maria* was rolling so fiercely from side to side that at times the mast would almost touch the crest of the waves. She was taking water. The sea was two foot over the port rails, thudding dully and repetitively against the cabin door.

Foster pushed against the throttle, trying to give the boat more power than she possessed.

She was making short darts forward in the troughs, then stopping and wallowing as she rose and the screw cleared the water.

She desperately needed to come around to the sea, but another wave across her bows and she might go under.

Her timbers were shrieking as Foster strained the rudder against the pressure of water on the keel.

Then quite suddenly she came into the lee of the island, into the choppy safe waters where the massive black cliffs shaded the sea in the glare of the lightning. Foster took her close in under the cliffs, leaving her just enough room to swing on the anchor.

Bill wrenched open the cabin door and went out into the rain to throw the stern anchor over. Foster waited until he felt the anchor grab, then cut the motor.

The *Santa Maria* swung around in the chop and seemed to be straining to get back to the rough seas that had almost drowned her.

'All right,' said Foster. 'Let's pump her out.'

15

The dawn broke clear and calm with the glassy green-blue sea contradicting any suggestion that a few hours before it had been a black and heaving malevolent thing.

Foster woke to a voice near his head saying, 'Are you the *Santa Maria*?'

He sat up on the deck and saw a small face with a white crown of hair peering over the starboard rail. Foster shook his head.

'Had a bad night, did you?' said the face. 'You're the *Santa Maria*, aren't you? Jack Foster?'

'That's right,' said Foster. He sat up and saw that the face was on the top of the body of a middle-aged man standing in a dinghy. Foster realised this must be the lighthouse keeper. He looked at the man cautiously. Lighthouse keepers sometimes had strange reputations.

Hadn't someone told him this man was peculiar. No, that had been the keeper of the Marabell light.

Bill woke and stared owlishly at the apparition on the starboard rail.

'I thought you must be the *Santa Maria*,' said the man. 'But your name plate isn't on.'

Foster looked over the side. The wooden panel that had borne the name of the *Santa Maria* was gone. He could see the holes left where the force of the water had torn the screws from the wood.

'Come ashore and have some breakfast,' said the man.

'Thanks,' said Foster. 'Just hang on a second while I take a look below.'

The floor of the cabin was still littered with glass from the shattered window. Foster took a torch and went down into the bilges. They had been pumped dry last night. There was an inch or two of water there now. A little more than usual, but nothing to worry about. Foster went back on deck and he and Bill climbed down into the dinghy.

'I'm John Gibbons,' said the man as he rowed the dinghy towards the stone wharf jutting out at the base of the cliffs. 'That was some storm last night, wasn't it? You out in it long?'

'Quite a while,' said Foster.

'You've been at sea for a few days, haven't you?' said Gibbons.

Foster wondered how much the man knew. Probably all there was to know.

'A week,' he said.

The dinghy nosed into the wharf. Gibbons threw a bow line over a bollard and shipped the oars. He led

Foster and Bill to a flight of steps up the cliffs.

'Yeah,' said Gibbons. 'They've been worried about you over at Bernadine.'

Foster thought of how Katey would have felt last night when the storm broke. She would have been awake too. Storms always made her nervous. He should have put a call through before he left the boat but it didn't matter, he could call from the lighthouse.

A herd of a couple of hundred goats moved away from them as they came to the top of the cliff. Most of the islands off the south coast were inhabited by goats. They were put there a hundred years ago or more by benevolent navigators with an eye to the wants of possible survivors of shipwrecks. Most of the herds were so inbred that many of the animals had five legs, or one too many horns.

'Take some goats' meat back with you if you want to,' said Gibbons. 'That lot want thinning out, getting too many billies.'

The white tower of the lighthouse seemed unrelated to the stark pointing column they had seen in the storm. The house itself, at the base of the column, was a solid stone building with wide verandahs around it.

'You by yourself here?' said Foster feeling a three-day growth of beard on his face.

'Yes,' said Gibbons. 'All alone.'

Their feet clumped on the wooden floor of the verandah.

'Been alone since the wife died. Come into the kitchen, we'll beat up some breakfast. But, hang on, we'd better call Bernadine first. I tell you what, you do that and I'll get the kettle on.' He showed Foster the radio and told him the call sign.

Foster got through to Armstrong at the police station.

'You're all right then, Jack?' said Armstrong.

'Yeah, we're all right, said Foster.

'Were you out in the storm?'

'For a while. We got in behind the island.'

'When are you coming back, Jack?'

'Soon,' said Foster.

'There's a lot of business waiting for you, you know, Jack.'

Foster could feel the constraint in Armstrong's voice.

'I know,' he said.

'You will be coming back eventually, won't you, Jack?'

'I'll be coming back,' said Foster. 'Listen, Rod, would you mind dropping in on Katey and telling her we're all right?'

'Sure, Jack. Jack, will you be staying on the island long?'

'No,' said Foster.

'Well, where will you be going? I mean, could I come out and meet you somewhere? I want to talk to you.'

'I'll see you when I get back,' said Foster.

'All right, Jack.'

'So long, Rod, over and out.'

Gibbons gave them steak and eggs.

'That meat might be a bit tough,' he apologised. 'I took it straight out of the deep freeze. You're supposed to let them thaw out first before you cook them.'

He poured their tea into fine bone china cups.

'First time I've had visitors in two months,' he said.

'Might as well put on a bit of a show, eh?'

Then he lit a cigarette and settled down to the exchange of gossip that was the lighthouse keeper's right.

'Tuna very late this year, I believe,' he said.

'Yes,' said Foster. 'Seen any about at all?'

'No,' said Gibbons. 'Not once this season. Not a ripple. Hear they got some further south though.'

'We got a couple of tons a fortnight back,' said Foster. 'None since.'

Gibbons poured himself another cup of tea.

'Well, I must say it's nice to have some company,' he said.

They heard the sound of an aeroplane overhead.

'Ah, there's the cannery plane,' said Gibbons. 'Good day for tuna today. Just the right temperature I'd say, about sixty-three.'

'Did you measure it?' said Foster.

'No,' said Gibbons. 'I reckon I can tell by the colour. When you've spent as long as I have just looking out at the sea you get to know a lot about it. I reckon that when she's just that shade of blue she is now she's just about right for tuna. It gets darker if it gets any hotter, and lighter when it's cooler. And even when there are clouds about, you know, there are sort of shades of grey and you can tell. It's hard to explain, it's more a feel about the colour than anything else. Would you like some more tea?'

'Thanks,' said Foster. He wanted to get back to his boat and out to sea again. He wanted to see whether she would take any water when she started to move. But the lighthouse keeper wanted to talk and he had a right to an audience.

'Yes,' said Gibbons expansively, leaning back in his chair, 'a lighthouse keeper gets to know the sea pretty well. You even start to talk to it after a while.'

Foster accepted this without surprise. It was generally accepted that a lighthouse keeper would be an eccentric. They stayed on the islands for months at a time, often longer, without a break. Many of them were alone, although some had families with them. A few of the lighthouses were maintained by two or even three families. It was sometimes better for those who were alone because they only had themselves to contend with. The tensions that arose when two or three families lived on an island had made legendary telling around the coast for many years.

'You like it out here by yourself?' said Foster conversationally.

'Oh, I don't know whether I like anything much,' said Gibbons. 'But you get used to it you know, besides I'm not exactly alone, there's the goats and the rabbits and the seals. They all make good company you know.'

The mild blue eyes looked out from under the white hair at Foster. 'I suppose you think I'm a little bit mad,' he smiled.

Foster shrugged. There was nothing you could say to a remark like that.

'You were having a bit of fun with some Italians I believe,' said Gibbons.

Now how the hell would he know about it, wondered Foster, he's just said he'd had no visitors to the island in two months. But there would have been the supply boat. He wouldn't count that as visitors. They would have told him.

'You could call it fun,' said Foster.

'And you're going to stay out until you actually get the tuna, eh?'

'That's the idea.'

'Well, I must say I admire your spirit. Yes, I do admire your spirit.'

Foster drank his tea and grunted.

'Reminds me of a little affair I had with the Italians myself last year,' said Gibbons.

Foster didn't care, but resigned himself to listening.

'I was having my holiday down at Landalar,' said Gibbons, 'and six Italian boats came in and moored in the port.

'Now, I mean to say, Landalar is a small port and six strange boats clutter it up pretty badly. Besides, the boats were bound to be fishing the breeding grounds.'

Foster was looking absently past Gibbons' shoulder out to the Pacific, a shiny vast silver lake in the morning sun.

'So,' said Gibbons, 'a couple of chaps and myself got together in the pub that night and decided to towel them up a bit.'

This exacted no comment from Bill or Foster. 'Towelling up' Italians was a patriotic duty for most of the fishermen along the coast.

'So we waited until about midnight and then we took a dinghy and rowed out to where these Italians were moored. I don't know whether you know Landalar?'

Foster and Bill grunted to indicate that they did.

'Then you know there's quite a current there and it runs straight down on to the breakwater.

'So, our idea was to cut the moorings and let the

Italians run down on the rocks. We thought they'd all be full of vino or whatever it is they drink and would run straight down on to the breakwater.'

Foster and Bill nodded. This would have been a reasonable plan. With any luck it would have caused considerable damage to the Italian boats without undue risk of actually killing anybody.

'So,' said Gibbons, 'out we row. And I come to the first boat and start quietly cutting through the mooring rope.

'Then, without a word of a lie, a light comes on and a bloody great dago leans over the bows and starts whacking into me with an oar.'

Foster didn't know whether he was supposed to laugh or sympathise, so he just grunted.

'And so we took off,' said Gibbons, 'and those Italians started up their boats and chased us all over the port . . . trying to ram us they were. We just managed to get ashore.

'But doesn't it just go to show what treacherous brutes they are: they must have been lying in wait for us!'

Foster and Bill finished their tea and escaped from Gibbons on the grounds that they had work to do on the boat.

Gibbons rowed them back to the *Santa Maria*.

'Drop in again for a meal anytime,' he said.

'Thanks,' said Foster.

'And keep on after those tuna.'

'I'll do that.'

'Don't let those Italians win. And remember, they're a treacherous lot.'

'I'll remember that.'

'So long then, Jack.'
'So long, John.'
'So long, Bill.'
'So long, John.'

16

They stayed in the shelter of the light island all that day cleaning up the *Santa Maria*. The yellow-tail they had caught a week before were all dead now and the stench enveloped the boat as the mid-day sun grew hot.

'We might as well chuck it out,' said Foster. 'We'll get some more here tonight.'

'Clean 'em out now?' said Bill.

'Leave it 'til dark in case the tuna show.'

Gibbons came across at lunch time and took them ashore for another meal. They stayed with him for a couple of hours and he helped them carry cans of water back to the *Santa Maria* to fill up the tanks.

At dusk they threw the dead bait overboard and swilled out the bait tanks with salt water. Gibbons lent them his dinghy and they made a haul of fresh bait in the bay.

163

Gibbons would have stayed to help them, but he had to tend the light. He came down when they had finished and took back his dinghy.

Foster and Bill slept on the bare decks that night because the bait net was wet.

The *Santa Maria* was encrusted with salt and the acrid tang probed into Foster's nostrils as he lay with his head on a blanket. It was different from the usual smell of scrubbed wood. . . .

It was a gun shot.

Foster woke up. It was daylight.

The gun sounded again, sharp above the little noises of the calm dawn.

Foster sat up. Bill was sitting on the deck looking bemusedly out to sea.

'What the hell's that?'

Another shot.

Foster looked up. Silhouetted against the sky at the top of the cliff he could see a man. It was Gibbons. It had to be Gibbons, there was no one else on the island.

What the hell was he doing?

Another shot.

Gibbons was waving and pointing the gun out to sea.

Foster leaped to his feet and ran up to the crow's-nest.

The sea to the east was a blinding sheet of silver in the dawn sun. To the north the silver faded into green and the green into dark blue.

There was a darker streak on the blue, a long moving streak like the touch of wind, but it wasn't wind, a dark thread a mile long.

'Tuna!' shouted Foster. 'Get that bloody anchor up,'

and he leapt from the crow's-nest to the deck, lurched into the cabin and started the motor.

Bill was hauling at the anchor rope and Foster turned the *Santa Maria* and ran over the anchor to clear it from the sand. Bill hauled it on to the deck as they headed into the open sea.

'Take the wheel,' shouted Foster. 'Keep her due north.'

From the crow's-nest he saw the ripple again . . . a mile long, more, almost motionless on the sea as though the wind had come just there and stopped.

There were thousands of fish in the school, thousands upon thousands of tuna moving slowly down the coast less than half a mile away.

The cannery plane came droning up from the south. Foster dropped back into the cabin and turned the radio on.

'Get the hatch covers off,' he said to Bill.

He saw the cannery plane bank and then spiral down when the pilot saw the vast patch of fish.

'Hello, Sid,' said Foster into the radio. 'I've spotted 'em. Jack Foster here.'

'Hello, Jack,' said the pilot. 'Everyone's been asking about you. Cannery boat on its way down to this patch too, but you'll get there twenty minutes before they do. Good luck.'

'Thanks, Sid.'

'You can see 'em all right, can you? Don't want me to hang around until you get there?'

'No thanks, Sid. I've got 'em.'

'Be seeing you.'

'Be seeing you.'

Bill dropped a fishing rack on either side of the *Santa*

Maria and took down a bait scoop.

He lifted the cover off the bait tank and stood with the scoop poised waiting until Foster ran the *Santa Maria* into the patch.

The shadow of fish barely moved. Foster steered straight for the centre. He could see the cannery boat off the northern horizon. They were welcome to what he left.

Over the edge of the shadow went the *Santa Maria* and Foster cut the motor back. He could see the fish now, two or three feet below the surface, sleek, powerful, poised in the water as though they were waiting for something to happen.

Foster switched the motor off.

'Bait!' he yelled and jumped out of the cabin, grabbed a pole, and fell into a fishing rack.

Bill scooped the first lot of bait over the side and at once the whole sea erupted in a hissing, foaming turmoil as the great tuna flung themselves on the yellow-tail.

Foster raised his pole and paused for a moment in an unconscious symbolic gesture. A flood of emotion akin to pure relief surged in his body and he flicked the squid down into the mouth of the one fish he somehow knew would take it among the hundred that threshed within his reach.

The fish rushed upwards towards the squid, caught it in its gaping, tooth-filled mouth, then kept on coming up out of the water, into the air, swinging around on the end of Foster's line, then losing the hook and dropping hard on the deck to lie there, drumming with glazing eyes and blood pouring from its gills.

The next fish was in the air already.

Bill threw in half a dozen scoops of bait then jumped into the stern rack and began poling.

'Come on tuna! Come on tuna!' muttered Foster, forcing himself to move his arms faster, flicking one hurtling fish free of the hook, cracking the line, dropping the squid to the sea again, drawing out the next fish before the first one hit the deck.

'Come on tuna, come on tuna!'

As he fished he tried to watch the edge of the seething water so the *Santa Maria* didn't drift free of it.

'More bait!' he shouted.

Bill dropped his pole and threw scoop after scoop of squirming yellow-tail into the turbulent mass of tuna. The frenzy of the fish seemed to reach an impossible crescendo as the two men stood on the rack and drew them out with the fast, graceful swing of shoulder and arms. The aft deck filled with vibrating, bloody fish. The blood was running under the rails, staining the water around the *Santa Maria*. The fish piled high, thudding one by one on to the vibrating mass already there and drumming out their lives in the hot morning air.

A voice came across the water, across the thrashing, hissing of the tuna, across the crack of the flailing lines, the thud and drumming fish in the boat.

'Hey, Jack. Do you want some help there?'

Foster turned without breaking the rhythm of his arms. The cannery boat was standing off twenty yards away.

'All you've got!' he yelled.

The cannery boat nosed forward and four men with poles in their hands jumped down to the deck of the *Santa Maria*. They fished from the sides, not bothering with fishing racks.

Six men fished in continuous action, each pulling thirty-five to forty pounds of tuna out of the water every two seconds. The air above the boat was filled with flying fish. They hit the deck so hard and fast the sounds of their fall merged into one almost unbroken roll. The tuna piled so high on the stern they began to topple over and slip back into the water. The men crowded up to the bows and fished shoulder to shoulder, hitting each other with their poles as they swung the tuna out of the water.

Fish slid down between the cabin and the side rails and piled up on the foredeck. The sea all around the *Santa Maria* turned pink with the blood that now poured red and thickly down her sides.

'Come on tuna! Come on tuna!'

The pile of tuna stood high on the foredeck but they were going over the sides again. Foster struggled over the mass of slippery, vibrating fish and forced open the door of the cabin.

'In here!' he yelled.

Foster and Bill stood side by side and pulled the fish straight out of the sea into the cabin.

'Shove them down the bilges,' screamed Foster when the cabin was filled.

The four men from the cannery boat watched in wonder as Bill pushed the fish down into the bilges, leaving more space for Foster to pull them into the cabin.

Foster worked in a controlled frenzy. Stripped to the waist, his body was thick with the blood of fish and still he poled. Fish filled the stern, the foredeck, the cabin, the bilges. Every man on the boat was standing on fish and still Foster poled. He pulled the tuna out and dropped them anywhere now because there was no space for them to go. Most of them slipped straight over the side again.

'Listen, mate,' shouted one of the men from the cannery boat. 'Lay off, you'll sink her.'

There were seventeen tons of tuna on board the *Santa Maria* and she was riding visibly lower in the water.

Foster stopped and drew his arm across his face, smearing away the blood through which he had been fishing blind for the last five minutes.

He looked around the *Santa Maria* and saw she could not hold another fish.

'All right,' he said. 'That'll do. She's yours.'

It was done. He had his tuna. Half an hour from the time he had heard the gunshot and it was done. He had what he wanted. In just half an hour.

The cannery boat moved in and began throwing bait overboard. The centre of the seething water moved over as the cannery men began fishing.

'Give me my men back,' shouted the skipper of the cannery boat.

Foster forced his way in among the fish in the cabin. Squatting on still living tuna, he started the motor and eased the *Santa Maria* towards the cannery boat. The four men leaped off and went straight to poling from the racks.

Foster turned the *Santa Maria* towards the west.

Bill came out of the bilges, slipping and scrambling on the fish that fell down from the cabin. He squatted beside Foster and tried to rub the blood off his arms.

'Good haul, Jack,' he said.

'Bloody marvellous!'

Foster did not think consciously at this moment. He sat on his fish, holding the wheel, full of a satisfaction and

169

fulfillment he could not put into words.

It was eight o'clock and he was about twenty-five miles from Bernadine. He'd be home in three or four hours.

The bows of the *Santa Maria* cut smoothly through the calm waters, but even the gentle movement sent two big tuna slithering off the pile on the foredeck into the water.

'Get out and see if you can stow those fish a bit better,' said Foster.

Bill slid out of the cabin, staggered, with his feet sinking in between the fish, up to the foredeck and began pushing the pile about so that it lay more evenly.

All the fish were dead now, but the wake of the *Santa Maria* was still pink with blood.

Foster turned on the radio and called up Rod Armstrong.

'Hello, Jack,' said Armstrong.

'Rod,' said Foster. 'I wonder if you'd do me a favour. Have you been to see Katey yet?'

'Not yet,' said Armstrong. 'I'm just going now.'

'Well, when you go down would you tell her I'm coming home and to do what I said about the cheque?'

'All right, Jack, I'll do that. What time are you coming in?'

'Should be there about midday,' said Foster. 'Rod, when you've given the message to Katey give us a call will you, to let us know everything's all right.'

'Sure, Jack.'

'And Rod, what's the weather forecast?'

'Wind and sea rising again this afternoon,' said Armstrong. 'You'll be right if you get back by midday. Should be all right anyway, it's not going to be too bad.'

'See you then, Rod.'

'See you, Jack.'

'Oh, and Rod, are you still there?'

'Yes, Jack.'

'Ring the cannery and ask them to have a truck down at the wharf about twelve, will you?'

'Got a good load, Jack?'

'Not bad,' said Foster. 'Be seeing you, Rod. Over and out.'

Bill came back into the cabin.

'She's riding very low in the water, Jack.'

'So would you if you were carrying seventeen tons of fish,' said Foster.

The wind was blowing through the broken window drying the blood on his body. He took a can of fresh water and poured it over his head, then tried to rub away the blood with his hands.

There were easily seventeen tons of fish on board, he thought. A clear thousand pounds' worth at the very least.

They couldn't touch him now.

He could pay off the boat and lay around for a couple of weeks while he got the keel fixed, then he'd have the whole of the rest of the season, another six weeks, to find the tuna again.

And next season?

Next season he'd have the whole run right through, with the *Santa Maria* free of debt.

Strange the way things happened. If that dago hadn't tossed himself over with the anchor Foster would never have had the *Santa Maria*.

And that, he thought, slapping the wheel affectionately

171

and moving his body to an easier position on the pile of fish, that would have been a pity.

Bill came through the cabin and went down to the bilges.

'I'll drag some of those fish down here, will I?' he said.

'I wouldn't bother,' said Foster. 'Only make them harder to get out. We can put up with this for a couple of hours. Is she taking any water?'

'There's a bit down here,' said Bill. 'It's hard to tell how much, it's full of fish. Not much I don't think.'

'You better pump it out.'

Bill came up and started turning the rotary pump.

'She probably sprung a bit along the keel you know,' he said. 'Not enough to worry about though.'

'We'll lay her up tomorrow and fix it,' said Foster. 'Or I might even keep her up and put on a new keel and garboards.'

'Um,' grunted Bill. 'I'd better put out the troll lines.'

'Relax, you stupid black bastard,' laughed Foster. 'We don't want any more fish on this boat.'

Bill laughed and settled back on the bed of fish to roll himself a cigarette.

A hundred gulls were screaming and wheeling around the stern of the *Santa Maria*, sweeping down to pick at the rigid bodies of the tuna.

Foster kept the radio on because he wanted to get the call from Armstrong when he had told Katey to do the business with the cheque.

He wondered whether the Italians would try to take the boat back when they landed. They'd know he was coming in by the time he arrived. Almost everybody on the coast would know it and they'd also know, in Bernadine anyway, that Katey had lodged the cheque. He might have a bit of trouble there yet. But the solicitor had said it would be all right.

The call from Armstrong came through at nine-thirty.

'I've seen Katey, Jack,' he said. 'She said everything was all right. I drove her down to the Courthouse myself.'

Foster laughed. 'Thanks, Rod,' he said.

He could hear the warmth in Armstrong's voice, a completely different tone from the one he'd used when Foster was on the edge of failure. Foster wondered how many people would be waiting on the pub verandah to watch him come across the bar with his thousand pounds' worth of fish.

By eleven o'clock the sea had begun to rise and the badly out of trim *Santa Maria* was wallowing her way through the low swell. The tide was running in and there would be a surf.

Foster wondered whether to go across the bar or put in at Landalar. He was four miles west of the Marabell light now and he could be home in an hour. It would take almost three hours to get down to Landalar. Still, he wasn't going through the surf with this load on if it looked at all bad.

He decided to go on and make up his mind when he could see the surf clearly. He had to remember to put a call through to get the cannery truck diverted, if he went down to Landalar.

Armstrong came on the radio again.

'Jack, could you pull in at Marabell and pick up a kid? Ron Benson's boy it is. He's pretty crook.'

'I'm loaded to the neck with tuna,' said Foster. 'Can't someone come out after him?'

'There's not a boat in the port,' said Armstrong. 'You're the closest for something like twenty miles. You'd better pick him up, Jack. The doctor here reckons it sounds like appendicitis.'

'Well, he's not going to be very comfortable with me,' said Foster.

'He's going to be a lot less comfortable if he stays on that island much longer.'

'Well, I'll do it,' said Foster. 'But I've got a hell of a lot of fish on board and I've got to come across the bar. It's no trip for a sick kid.'

'It's the only way we can get him off at the moment,' said Armstrong. 'Unless we get the helicopter from Nowra and that'll take a couple of hours.'

'All right, I'll get him,' said Foster.

He changed course slightly to come around to the bay at Marabell. The sea was rising, although it was still only a long smooth swell.

But as they rounded the island Foster saw that waves were breaking on the sand in the bay and against the small stone wharf.

'Damn this for a joke,' he said. 'If I go in through that I'm just as likely not to get out.'

Two men were walking down the path from the lighthouse towards the wharf. One of them was carrying a bundle which Foster assumed was the sick boy.

Still, somebody had to go in, he thought. The fish he was carrying wouldn't make much difference to the handling of the boat, so it might as well be him. Except that no other boat had a cobra-riddled keel. He couldn't take too many knocks on the wharf.

'Listen, Bill,' he said. 'I'll tell you what we'll do. I'll

take her straight into the bay and nose her up to the wharf. You get a line from the bows to the wharf. I'll let the stern swing round and hold her off with the rudder and as soon as they get the kid on board throw off the bow line and I'll take her straight out.'

The waves running into the bay weren't bad but it was not a situation a man would normally take a boat into.

It'd be a hell of a bloody thing to lose it all now, thought Foster.

He called Armstrong.

'Rod,' he said. 'There's a bit of a sea running into the bay here. I'm going to have to get that kid off pretty quickly. It's going to be a bit risky for the kid as well as me. Are you sure it's worth a try?'

'I've got the doctor here, Jack, I'll let him talk to you.'

'Jack, it's Rex Clayton here.'

'Receiving you, doc,' said Foster.

'Jack, it's hard to tell you what to do in a situation like this. From what they've told me on the island the kid could have a bad appendix. It wouldn't be wise to leave him unattended for long, but I can't tell what the situation is out there. If there's any grave risk of hurting him getting him on board, well, then, you better not try. I'm afraid it's your decision, Jack. All I can say is that if he can be got off quickly he should be got off quickly.'

'O.K. doc,' said Foster. 'I'll go and get him.' There wasn't much else a man could do, he thought ruefully, when it was put to him like that.

'You better clear some of those fish out of the cabin into the bilge and make a bit of space for the kid,' Foster said to Bill. 'If those blokes are coming with him they'll just have to sit on the fish.'

Bill cleared one corner of the cabin.

Foster stood the *Santa Maria* off the bay for a few minutes studying the movement of the water. It wasn't too bad. In normal circumstances he wouldn't have thought twice about it. As it was . . . well, hell, a man had to live with himself.

'All right, Bill, go up front,' said Foster. 'We'll go in and get him.'

He took the *Santa Maria* slowly into the bay, heading directly for the wharf. The two men were standing on the wharf now and Foster could see the boy wrapped up in a blanket sitting on a suitcase.

The waves were breaking across the end of the wharf. That meant the boy would have to jump or be thrown across the foot or two of water.

God help him if he fell between the *Santa Maria* and the solid stone wall.

Bill was standing on the bows straddling the pile of fish with a rope in his hands. The *Santa Maria* nosed towards the wharf. A wave caught her and took her ahead too fast. Foster put the throttle into idle and the gear into reverse, holding her back.

She rolled in a trough and Foster cursed as he saw a couple of tuna slide off the foredeck straight down into the water. They went in cleanly like spears and disappeared. Dead tuna don't float.

He put the gear into forward again and the *Santa Maria* went up to the wharf.

Bill threw the bow line to one of the men standing there and he looped it over a bollard.

Foster brought the throttle back and the stern of the *Santa Maria* began to come round. He turned the wheel to starboard and gave her a little power, working the rudder against the pull of the bow line and the thrust of the sea.

She came right around until she was parallel with the wharf, held at the bows by the line and at the stern by the action of the screws and rudder.

One of the men threw a suitcase into the cabin. The boy was standing on the edge of the wharf waiting to jump.

He didn't look particularly sick, thought Foster.

'Come on!' he shouted.

One of the men jumped across the two feet of water between the wharf and the rising *Santa Maria*. He climbed on to the cabin roof and held his hand out to the boy.

The boy grabbed the hand and jumped but slipped and fell down between the wharf and the boat.

The man was still holding his hand.

A wave picked up the *Santa Maria* and Foster, in one suspended agonised moment of time, foresaw the two things that could happen within the next four seconds: he could hold the *Santa Maria* where she was and the boy would be crushed flat between the heavy planking of the boat and the stone wharf, or he could swing the stern out and the next wave would drop the *Santa Maria*'s bows against the stone wharf.

He swung the wheel over hard and gunned the motor. The stern came away and the bows hit the wharf with a sharp crack.

The man struggling with the boy toppled forward and leaped across to the wharf to save himself going into the water. He was still holding the boy's hand as he fell down on the wharf. The other man knelt down and helped hold the boy up. They were both elderly men and made heavy weather of it.

Bill leaped across from the bows on to the wharf to help them. The *Santa Maria* swung out until she was at right angles to the wharf, still held by the bow line.

Foster kept the engines in reverse.

The boy was hauled up on the wharf and one of the elderly men raised both hands above his head and crossed them and uncrossed them.

They didn't want to try boarding the *Santa Maria* again.

Bill had been holding the bow line on a couple of turns around the for'd bollard and now, as the *Santa Maria* backed away, the line slipped free.

Foster turned the wheel hard to starboard and turned into the waves. Bill would have to stay there. Foster wasn't going into the wharf again.

He ran the *Santa Maria* out of the bay under full throttle and headed towards the Bernadine bar. Then he took a torch from a locker and went down to the bilges to see what damage the wharf had done.

Three layers of fish were lying on the bottom of the boat. Foster pulled away a couple from the top and found the lower two layers were already covered with water. The blow on the bows had sprung the garboard planks.

Foster clawed the tuna aside and tried to get to the leak.

The *Santa Maria* lost course and turned across the waves.

She gave a lurch and Foster was flung in a sprawl over the tuna. A sharp fin cut his face.

He scrambled back to the cabin and brought the *Santa Maria* around to the sea again.

The bar was three miles away. It would take him a little under half an hour to get there.

Armstrong came through on the radio. 'Did you get the kid, Jack?'

'No,' said Foster. 'Too rough.'

'Are you going to try again?'

'No, damn it,' said Foster. 'I'm sinking.'

'What happened?' said Armstrong sharply.

'I hit the wharf and . . . oh, what's it matter? I'm coming in. Be seeing you.'

'Hold on, Jack. You better go down to Landalar if you can, there's a bit of surf over the bar.'

'I haven't got time,' said Foster bitterly. 'I'm sinking I tell you. Be seeing you.'

He left the wheel again and grabbed a gaff hook from the rack outside the cabin. Standing on top of the ladder to the bilges he gaffed the tuna out one by one, trying to clear a space in the bows where the leak would be worst.

He dropped the tuna out through the broken glass in the cabin window on to the foredeck. Most of them slid deftly over the side and dropped neatly and cleanly head first into the water.

Foster could see the water in the bilges now, black and oily, swirling backwards and forwards as the *Santa Maria* headed towards the bar.

He grabbed a pile of clothing from a locker and dropped down into the water. It was up to his knees. He felt along the garboard planks and found a gap almost as wide as his fingers and stuffed a shirt into it. He was feeling for another gap when the *Santa Maria* swung around in the sea again. A dozen tuna slithered forward around his legs. He climbed back up into the cabin and brought the bows around.

The bar was only a mile away.

Foster could see the white line of the surf. It was high, too high, but there was nowhere else he could go. The *Santa Maria* would stay afloat until she reached the surf. He didn't think he would have time to get up the river. He would try to ride straight across the surf and beach her on the sands.

He could see the hotel now. There were twenty or more people on the verandah looking down at him.

Foster called the police station. 'I'm taking water fast,' he said. 'I'm going to run straight in through the surf and try and catch a roller on to the beach. Would you try and get a few blokes to come around and help me get the fish off? And get Jenkins to bring his bulldozer over.'

'Jack,' said Armstrong. 'If you've got a big load of fish on and you're taking water you'll be riding very low. It's only half tide. You'd be lucky to have five foot of water over the bar.'

'I know that,' said Foster.

'Can you get down to Landalar? You might have a better chance.'

'I won't stay afloat another half-hour,' said Foster. 'Will you get those men down there?'

'Sure, sure, Jack. I'll fix that,' said Armstrong soothingly. 'But, Jack, what weight fish have you got on board?'

'Seventeen tons,' said Foster bitterly.

'And how much water?'

'I don't know, a foot or two,'

There was a pause.

'Jack,' said Armstrong. 'Listen. You better start throwing those fish overboard. You'd never get across with

180

that on, much less the water. Don't be a bloody fool altogether man, you'll kill yourself.'

'Well,' said Foster. 'Pity! Over and out.'

The *Santa Maria* was wallowing badly.

Foster thought about trying to block the leak again but there was no point in it. He would be in the surf in five minutes. The water he'd take on now wouldn't make that much difference and he would lose time if the boat swung off course.

He pushed hard against the throttle but the engine was already flat out.

Over the port rail he could see the water unusually close. The *Santa Maria* was riding at least a foot lower than she should. She had a four-foot draught normally. Five feet now. Probably five and a half feet by the time he hit the surf. The water was five feet over the bar. Seven or eight or ten feet under when a big wave went across. He had to get on to a big wave and ride it across.

Three minutes to the surf. Foster looked through the broken glass of the cabin window at the glistening fish piled high on the bows; at the long line of the coast stretching away to the north; at the town crouching on the hills; at the hotel overlooking the bar; at the drinkers standing, glasses in their hands, watching the drama on the blue-green water below.

He could leave the boat and swim in from here easily. If he took her across and hit the bar the chances were she would roll over on him. He didn't even consider leaving.

Taking a knife from the rack in the cabin he jammed the cabin door to make sure it would stay open. He wanted to be able to get out if he had to.

Foster counted the waves: a small one, a small one,

another small one, a big one. Not big enough, but the biggest he'd get.

For once in his life he wished the surf was higher so he could throw the *Santa Maria* on to the crest of a great foaming breaker which would launch her high on to the sand.

A small wave, a small wave, another small wave and then a big one.

That was it. One in four and the fourth one was not quite big enough.

He swung the bows around pointing into the surf, the throttle back. A small wave rolled under him and the stern of the *Santa Maria* sank desperately low as it went past.

A second small wave went under and half a dozen fish slipped over the side.

A third small wave; Foster pushed the throttle forward slightly and as the fourth wave, the big one, rolled up behind him he gunned the motor and sent the sluggish *Santa Maria* heaving forward towards the bar.

The wave gathered behind him.

He saw the sun glinting through it.

He felt the stern lift involuntarily. His hand thrust hard against the extended throttle.

The centre of the wave moved forward.

The *Santa Maria* rose.

The wave broke.

The bow of the *Santa Maria* thrust half out into the sunlit air and she soared, light now even under her burden of fish and water, towards the sand a hundred yards away across the bar.

One moment of pure exaltation gripped Foster as he

stood there holding the living wheel, his legs straddling the tuna, feeling the *Santa Maria* alive, feeling the bows thrust high from the creaming water, feeling the rush of air through the broken window, cool on his face.

The keel hit the bar.

The *Santa Maria* stopped almost dead.

The wave rushed on and left her. Her bows thumped down into the sand.

Foster was flung forward across the wheel and banged his head against the window.

The fish in the cabin fell forward against his body.

He saw half a ton of tuna fall off the bows.

Foster threw himself back and tried to stand up against the weight of fish pushing against him.

He still had his hand on the throttle and the *Santa Maria* was moving forward dragging her keel through the sand. But the sand was working on the rudder too and she was broaching, coming around slowly broadside to the sea. Foster flung his whole weight on the wheel trying to pull the dead-weight of the *Santa Maria* round by the rudder.

The next small wave came through and she moved another two or three feet across the bar but she was broaching further.

The rudder was deep in the sand and not all of Foster's strength on the wheel could move it.

Fifteen feet away the sea foamed in the deep water across the bar.

On the next small wave the boat rose, wallowed a couple of feet further and dropped again, almost side on to the waves now.

The motor was thudding violently.

Another wave and the boat was sliding grudgingly across the bar. She made five feet broadside to the sea.

Foster could see the deep water eight feet from the port rails. He grabbed the wheel spokes in his hands and threw the whole might of his shoulders and body to drag her around to the port.

Then the fourth wave, the big one, came through and crashed on to the stern deck of the *Santa Maria*, dropping ten tons of water in with the weight of the fish and the water in the bilges.

The *Santa Maria* stuck like a hundred tons of lead on the bar.

For a moment, as the wave rolled on past, she was half out of the water, her solid lines motionless in the wide blue-green trough behind the wave.

Foster turned to throw himself out the cabin door but fell in the moving mass of fish under his feet.

Another wave drove over and the water crashed into the cabin and down into the bilges.

Something hit Foster heavily on the head.

Water poured into his nose and mouth.

Choking, he dragged himself to his feet and threw himself at the doorway as the next wave, a big one, hit.

The ropes holding the diesel drums on the stern deck broke. The wave picked up the drums and dashed them against the cabin. The cabin splintered apart and the drums went through and knocked Foster down.

He went under the water in the cabin of his own boat.

The drums kept going and went out through the front windscreen, completely demolishing the remains of the cabin. The boat was full of water and Foster was swirled around in a flurry of dead tuna.

Then the water drained away and he came up and scrambled out through the wreckage of the cabin on to the stern deck.

He felt the *Santa Maria* swell as she burst open like a melon.

Foster sank in the storm of wreckage and as he went down he saw, like shapes in a nightmare, a stream of tuna slipping away from the foredeck into the surf.

He flung himself sideways to clear the wreckage and was stopped abruptly in his plunge by something holding his toe. He fell flat into the water alongside the burst bull with his right foot held taut by something through his toe. He spun around in the water like a lure on the end of a tuna troll line.

In that moment Foster knew that a hook from one of the tuna poles had gone through his toe. The pole was caught in the wreckage. He was hooked on the end of a line with a breaking strain of two hundred pounds

The wave washed past him and his left leg found the sand. He hopped forward through the water trying to relieve the strain on his toe and pull out the hook.

The barbless hook that slipped so easily from the mouth of the flying tuna was stiffly caught in the flesh of a man.

Another wave came past and knocked him flat on his back spinning him around again and drawing his head under.

He broke the surface and stretched out towards the shore feeling downwards for the sand with his left foot. He turned around and tried to pull himself back to get the pressure off the line but another wave was rolling towards him.

'Christ!' screamed Jack Foster. He had lost his boat, did he have to drown as well?

'Christ!'

The wave hit him and he went under again struggling like a striped tuna dragged behind a boat, his scream, half prayer, half blasphemy, choked in his throat by foaming salt water. The water tried to drag him towards the shore and he spun around on the end of the line. Water swirled down his nose. His open eyes saw the chaos of green and white begin to go red.

Then the flesh of his toe gave way and the wave carried him across the bar.

He went down deep and came up dazed and sick.

Languidly, not caring, he swam towards the sand and saw for the first time that his left forearm was cut to the bone from the elbow to the wrist.

The wound gaped red as he raised his arm for a stroke, then came out of the water clean and white, then went red.

His arms hit the sand and he crawled forward. Somebody grabbed him by the shoulders and darkness happened to him.

In the darkness he could hear voices and somewhere above them, and above the sound of the surf, the sharp, harsh cries of seagulls.